Pat Riordan and his feisty assistant, Reiko Masuda, are back again . . . involved in what *might* be a plot to assassinate the Pope, a nasty bit of business with a seedy paramilitary group, a manuscript alleged to have been written by one of the nineteenth century's greatest authors, and a frankly dishonest stockbroker who seeks refuge in the bed of a female cello player from the San Francisco Symphony.

Another adventure in the life of the reluctant, whimsical Riordan finds him accepting Reiko as a full partner. If you've ever visited the Monterey Peninsula of California, you'll recognize where all this intense activity takes place. If not, you might want to go there some day.

POETS
NEVER
KILL

Other books by this author:
Chinese Restaurants Never Serve Breakfast
Live Oaks Also Die

Roy Gilligan

POETS NEVER KILL

Brendan Books
San Jose, CA

Art direction by Robin Gilligan
Cover art by Reed Farrington
Photography by SplashStudios
Book design and typography by Jim Cook/Santa Barbara

Manufactured in the United States of America.

  1 — 91

Library of Congress Catalog Card Number: 90-92285
ISBN 0-9626136-1-4

AUTHOR'S NOTE

It's possible that you may take the contents of this book seriously, and believe that all of these characters did all of these things during the memorable autumn of 1987. Set your mind at rest. The Pope *did* visit the Monterey Peninsula. The stock market *did* go down the tubes, temporarily. The characters are all more or less based on people I know, have known, would like to know, or would just as soon forget. But any resemblance? Perish the thought.

Reed Farrington again did the cover, and my favorite child, Robin, directed the art. That's what an art director does, isn't it? The picture of me on the back of the book remains the same. It's a fair likeness, and you're going to see it again and again. Photographs never lie, but paintings are forever.

Cheryl Yemoto was at my side to pass on the proper Japaneseness of Reiko. My wife, Jane, was at my other side, urging me on to bigger and better things. And I can never forget the help and encouragement I have received from the World's Greatest Cartoonist (Retired), Gus Arriola, and his beautiful wife, Frances.

POETS NEVER KILL

1

I've been doing a lot of walking on the beach

IT'S LIKELY that you don't remember the Pope's visit to Carmel. It made quite a stir on the Monterey Peninsula back in '87. But a lot of what happened during the visit of the supreme VIP of the Roman Catholic Church was pretty hush-hush. Until now.

I was involved in my usual tangential fashion in certain bizarre happenings that were not supposed to see the light of day until a sufficient amount of time had passed. It wasn't really left up to my good judgment, but I think I can tell the story now. It has a lot to do with the Pope's visit, but what got me involved was the death of a client who...hey, but I'm getting ahead of myself. It all started on an uneventful day at the end of summer:

I was walking on Carmel Beach thinking of Helen. I do that often, even now, years after her death. You've heard me speak of her, my wife, my one and only wife. She was a tough, honest, loving creature who worked in what she referred to as "the rag trade." She took fashion seriously, and she was very good at what she did. She died in 1976 in the prime of her life on Highway 280 as it runs through San Bruno, just south of San Francisco.

Helen is on my mind as I walk on Carmel Beach because it was she who introduced me to Robinson Jeffers. Not the man, of course, who died in the early sixties, but his poetry, mainly about this spectacular stretch of Calfornia coast from here to Morro Bay, through the Big Sur country.

She insisted that the poet's ghost still walks the beach, especially when the fog is in and the wind is up, just as the man did regularly when he lived. She took me to Tor House on Carmel Point, which stood alone on the brushy shore for years. The stonemason who built the original house for Jeffers took the poet on as a day laborer and taught him, in Jeffers' words, "to make stone love stone." Jeffers himself then built the tower and it stands proudly still. Tourists are invited to visit this shrine to California's most gifted and controversial poet. Thousands do, every year.

The visitors inspect the house and garden. They are shown the house dog's grave, and somebody might read the poem that has brought tears to any dog lover's eyes, including mine. They climb the tower on the outside, and are shown the hidden inner passage down that has triggered claustrophobia in me more than once. It's an inspirational tour for nearly everyone. Everyone except a client of mine, a Carmel lawyer named Gravesend who, the sheriff's office thinks, fell or was pushed off the tower and smashed his skull.

Which is why I was walking on Carmel Beach in the first place.

When Howard Gravesend came to my office on Alvarado Street in Monterey a matter of hours before his death, he seemed to be in good spirits. He was a robust, pink-faced fellow, about fifty, a hail-fellow, quick with the latest bit of gossip, or the current socially acceptable dirty joke. I had worked with him a few times, even before I moved my office from San Francisco to Monterey. Howard did some legal work for George Spelvin (fictitious name), a wealthy Pebble Beach social type, who was responsible for bringing me down here.

Howard always burst through the door with a big "hello" in a voice that vibrated the frosted glass in the partition, and caused Reiko to rise from her chair in terror. You'd think by this time she'd have got used to the colorful characters that come to my door, but Howard had ways of varying his approach to keep her off guard. Most of them were not very original or imaginative, running as they did to the use of, say, a phony nose and Groucho moustache attached to a pair of fake spectacles.

Anyhow, Howard came noisily into the office, Reiko reacted by throwing a plastic souvenir back-scratcher from Disneyland at him, and I grabbed him by the hand and led him into my more or less private office, which is just a bit smaller than Reiko's. ("You don't need much room," she says. "You never *do* anything.")

"You appear to be in good spirits, Howard."

"I am, Riordan, I am. I have learned this morning that an uncle I hardly knew has departed this earth and left me a fair chunk of cash. *And* Joanna has decided to divorce me."

He beamed. Howard's red face seemed a bit redder than usual, there was a certain tenseness around the eyes and mouth, and he drummed his fingers on the arm of my only guest chair.

"Did Joanna know that you had this windfall when she made her announcement?"

"Nope. She's not *gonna* know. Until after she gets the divorce."

"How are you going to keep it from her, man? There are laws in this state. You know that as well as anyone."

"Listen, this uncle of mine was a manipulator. His legal residence was an island in the West Indies. You can get away with *anything* from there."

I had serious doubts. Howard Gravesend had always been straight with me. I had done investigative work for him for the better part of ten years. But he didn't seem to be quite the same guy that morning.

"I'm puzzled, Howard. What do you want *me* to do? I assume that this is more than a friendly visit."

"Check out Joanna for me." The grin of elation left his face, and he frowned. "I can't afford to leave anything to chance. She knows *I've* been messin' around. I want to find out what she's been doin'."

Aha, I thought, it's the old pot versus kettle ploy. Not uncommon in divorce cases. I've worked on quite a few of them. They're usually not very interesting, nor are they much fun. A couple of people who get sick of each other and seek freedom through fornication. Takers, not givers.

"I'm not so sure I want this case, Howard. I've known Joanna as long as I have known you. If I start snooping around after her, she'll spot me in a minute. Besides, she's a friend of Sally's."

Sally Morse is my own current "significant other," a designation I dislike, however apt it may be. We enjoy each other's company and we sleep together regularly. I don't know if there's an official name for that.

"You're the only investigator I trust, Riordan. You've gotta do it." Howard's expression changed to one of pleading. He had a pendulous lower lip, and he looked at that moment like a rather chubby hound dog.

"OK. I'm not sure about how I'm going to get the job done. I've never followed an acquaintance before. Joanna's a fine figure of a woman and it'd be a real pleasure to observe her from the rear anytime. But I still think she'll spot me if I try to trail her."

"Just ask around, Riordan. Monterey's a small town, man. Here, I've written down some of the places she likes to go. *And,* some people she's been seen with."

He handed me a sheet of stationery from his law office with the names of half a dozen restaurants and bars typed on it. Below the typing, in Howard's almost illegible hand, were the names of three prominent citizens. A glance told me I was familiar with them all, and the name of one of them startled me.

"Him? Joanna's been seen with *him?*"

"Well, not really. But she's seen all his movies. And she shook hands with him once at a fund raiser in Carmel."

I drew a line through the name. The other two were equally familiar to me, but not internationally recognizable like the first. One was Howard's law partner, Alden Crowley. The other was an author of suspense novels that sold quite well. The latter I knew only slightly, but admired to a certain degree. That is, I admired the guy's work. Michael Flaherty (legally changed from Elroy Finch) had, I knew, been born in Fresno and strayed no further out of California than Las Vegas, but he wrote with enormous flair of Cairo, Istanbul and Moscow. I had read four or five of his books but I could not tell you now what any one of them was about. I only know that I was fascinated in the process of reading.

Howard Gravesend left my office that morning pretty happy. "Be good, Riordan," he said as he left, "the Pope's comin' next month." In a day he was dead. His uncle's "fortune" was in limbo. And Joanna was involved in a pretty weird situation.

I've been doing a lot of walking on the beach.

2

"I'm Joanna's attorney."

I S THE loudmouth gone?"

Reiko stuck her head through my door and peered into all corners of the room.

"He must have passed you on the way out, Reiko-san."

"Oh, no. I went over to Lenny's office just after that nerdy lawyer got here. I cannot stand the man. I can't stand the lousy coffee Lenny always forces on me, either, but you know, the much lesser of two evils."

Lenny is a kid who works in the accounting office next door. He has had a thing for Reiko ever since we moved in, although I suspect he's a few years younger than she is. Reiko's a cool thirty-six or so but, like most Japanese, she doesn't seem to age from year to year. At least, that's the way it looks to most of us whose ancestors came from across the other ocean. She and Lenny are kids to me, though. I'll come right out and say I'm something over fifty, but not how much. Anybody who calls me a "senior citizen" will get a punch in the mouth.

"Howard Gravesend is a client, a paying client. Unlike others who have commissioned my services, he has paid on time, every time. Don't put him down."

"I still don't like him." She pushed her lips into a pout and sat on the edge of my desk. "What does he want?"

I told her briefly what Howard had asked us to do.

"You're going to chase around after Joanna Manning Gravesend, the bitch goddess of Monterey society? You're nuts, Riordan."

"Wait a minute. I'm only going to do what Howard has asked me to do. Check her out."

"Check her out in the sack? I hear she's got round heels."

"You don't know a goddam thing!" I said, heatedly, although I suspected that Reiko knew more than I did about a lot of things. "I've known Joanna for a long time. Ah, fairly well. She's a . . . a classy lady."

"Bullshit, Riordan," said Reiko as she flounced out of the room.

I kicked back in my foam and plastic upholstered swivel chair and put my feet up on my desk.

The first work I did for Gravesend and Crowley was on a consumer fraud case. Their client was accused of misrepresenting a beauty product that would take years off a woman's age. What it really did was take a layer of skin off her face. My job, I think, was to try to find women who would testify on the defendant's behalf. Aside from a seventy-eight-year-old lady in Carmel Valley who giggled on the stand, I struck out. Plaintiff got a pretty good judgment, as I recall.

The guy who actually hired me was Alden Crowley. He paid me a nice fee with a smile, even though I hadn't done him much good.

"We didn't think we could win, Pat. We knew the guy was a snake oil peddler from 'way back. But his checks were good."

After that I did little jobs for the firm fairly regularly, routine stuff, boring stuff. The stuff that pays the rent and the light bill, and backs the monthly checks for Reiko's computer, which has grown like that awful plant in *Little Shop of Horrors*, and is just as frightening to me. Why she needs all that additional hardware is a complete mystery.

But Howard had engaged me to investigate his partner as a possible co-respondent. I thought that was pretty juicy.

I called Sally.

"Morse Travel, how may I help you?"

"Let me count the ways . . . "

"Don't get concupiscent on the telephone, Riordan."

"Sally, I am about to lay some confidential information on you.

Before I do, however, I must insist that you take a vow not to reveal a word. . . ."

"For God's sake, get to the point."

"All right, here it is: Howard Gravesend has hired me to check up on Joanna. *She's* going to divorce *him,* but he wants some info to avoid having her getting his underwear along with his pants. What do you know?"

There was a silence. Then:

"I knew it was going to happen. They were light years apart. Howard was out to hump every woman over eighteen on the Peninsula. He did like to keep it legal, you know. *And* I think Joanna was having her amusement—although I really don't know who the man, or men, is, or are. She's been pretty discreet."

"So far, ma'am, you've told me what I already know. Which ain't gonna do me much good. Why don't I come out to your place tonight for a plate of spaghetti? And a little hanky panky."

"Why does working on unfaithful spouse cases make you so horny? Not tonight, Riordan. I'm making a presentation to a group over at the Doubletree. Very extensive tour. Very big money."

"I'm crushed. Guess I'll just hop down to the video store and rent a Kim Basinger movie. I always turn the sound off. Kim has a lot to say to me when she just *moves.*"

"Tomorrow night, pal. And save your strength, you're not as young as you once were. Bye."

I visualized Sally as I hung up the phone. She's a good-sized woman, almost as tall as I am, and *zaftig.* An old word for it is "statuesque." She wears her hair short and neat and describes it as "naturally curly and prematurely gray," although I'm inclined to think her language is cosmetic.

Sally is the first woman to come along since Helen died who fulfills my notion of what female companionship ought to be. She's completely feminine, independent, tough, sentimental, funny, intelligent, and sexy. I have actually heard myself suggesting that we get married, or, at least, live together.

"Maybe some day, Pat. Right now, and in the forseeable future, I think you'd be under foot too much. You'd object to panty hose hanging in the shower stall. You'd expect me to fix your breakfast.

Which I don't mind for a couple of days in a row. But not a lifetime. Not now. But . . . who knows? I might change my mind."

Sally was married for a while to a trumpet player who is now a studio musician in Hollywood, making a good living recording background music for TV shows. I've met him a couple of times. He's quite a philosopher for a guy called "Jimmy," a typical musician with his heart in his work and his hair in his eyes. I'm sure he loved Sally—probably still does—but her attitude toward him now is strictly maternal. He shows up at her place in Carmel Valley, she pats him on the head and sends him back to L.A.

What to do about Joanna Gravesend? I gave the matter some serious thought. She had announced her intention to divorce Howard. I wondered how many other people knew about it.

I swung my feet down off the desk and called Alden Crowley.

His secretary told me he was on another line with a client, and I said I'd hold. I was treated to a chunk of the score from *The Sound of Music.* Only a New Yorker like Oscar Hammerstein could believe that "fa" was a "long, long way to go."

When Crowley came on the line, he was less than cordial.

"What can I do for you, Riordan?"

"Your partner told me his wife is divorcing him. Who's her lawyer?"

"That's a pretty shitty question. Are you working for Howard? Or do you fancy working for Joanna?"

Crowley is inclined to affect a few Briticisms, like using "fancy" as a verb.

"Sorry, Alden. Didn't mean to upset you. You and Howard are still good friends, I take it."

Crowley's tone softened. "Well, maybe not good friends. We *work* well together, but—we've . . . never been all that compatible *personally.* You understand."

I understood. Alden Crowley and Howard Gravesend were an odd couple in one of the odder senses. Crowley is quiet, tight-lipped, meticulous. I've already told you enough about Gravesend.

It was at Crowley's insistence that they moved their office from Monterey to a suite just off Carmel Rancho Boulevard in what has been referred to as "Greater Carmel-by-the-Sea." This is pretty funny. The actual village—whose mayor at the time of the Pope's visit was a movie star who specializes in roles which require him to dispose violently of a minimum of a dozen bad guys—is only one mile square. Alden wanted a touch of Carmel chic on the firm's stationery and a Carmel prefix on the phone number. Howard, though a brilliant lawyer, lacked what Alden might call "style." He invariably ordered the steak and lobster combination ("surf and turf") in restaurants, and would argue that Peewee Herman is a comic genius.

I decided to go for broke.

"Alden, is there—or has there been—anything going on between you and Joanna?"

He laughed, rather harshly, I thought. "Sure, Riordan. To answer your original question, I filed the suit for divorce this morning. *I'm* Joanna's attorney."

3

"I want to be your partner now."

WHETHER OR NOT a man can be both a lawyer and a co-respondent in a divorce case is not a question for me to answer. But Crowley's announcement was enough to cause me to regard him as something of a long shot as Joanna's paramour.

That whittled Howard's list down to one: the author, Michael Flaherty. Flaherty has done well financially with his books, several of which have been best-sellers. One, at least, was made into an expensive but only moderately successful motion picture that attempted to follow all the plotlines in the book religiously, and sent audiences out into the night in total confusion. I remember seeing it with Sally at the Golden Bough in Carmel. All I can recall of the evening is that the popcorn was too salty.

However, Flaherty was wealthy enough to own a house on the west side of San Antonio Street with more than what the local real estate folks call "a peek at the ocean." He lived alone in the five bedroom, two-story place, after a second divorce. Both of his wives had been independently wealthy. The first one had supported him for years while he wrote two or three long, unpublishable Great American Novels. When in frustration he turned to the world of international sex and intrigue, the money started pouring in, and wife number one, having served her purpose, was quietly phased out. I have never been quite sure what happened to number two.

Despite his success with spy novels, Flaherty liked to boast of his talents as a poet. He was a fierce admirer of Robinson Jeffers and an active member of the group that supported Tor House. As a Jeffers fan myself, I had met Flaherty at gatherings where he liked to read the poet's work in a large doomsday voice that had a three tone range, from somber to sepulchral.

I've always been sort of fascinated by authors of fiction. Like, where does all that stuff come from? I cornered Flaherty one evening at a conclave of Jeffers admirers. He is a big, shaggy man with an enormous amount of unruly gray hair and a beard that makes it unnecessary for him ever to wear a necktie. With his great nose and bushy eyebrows arching over bright black eyes, he looks like Jeff Corey playing "John Brown."

The conversation, as I remember it, went like this:

"Mr. Flaherty, I'm Pat Riordan. I've always admired your work."

"So have I, Riordan. But the good stuff doesn't sell. The bullshit sells. The bullshit *sells*. Now, *Jeffers*—that's *great* stuff, don't you know. Too bad he had such bad press late in his career. The man was a bloody genius. Don't you think I ought to play him in the movies?"

I couldn't bring myself to mention that Jeffers was clean shaven, and I'd always envisioned Fritz Weaver in the part. Flaherty's ego had stunned me for a moment. But I managed to go on.

"Mr. Flaherty—"

"Call me Mike, Riordan. It's a phony name, anyhow." He opened his large mouth and laughed loudly. "Pat and Mike, by God! Once there were these two Irishman. Haw, haw, haw!"

I smiled nervously. "What I wanted to ask you, Mike, is, well, how do you get the inspiration for those complicated plots you use in your books?"

"That is the question every goddam newspaper and magazine interviewer always asks. I guess it's a good enough question. A lot more civilized than the stuff those godawful TV people come up with." The tone was one of disgust, but there was a smile tugging at his lips. His voice dropped to a whisper. "I *steal* 'em, Riordan. I *steal* 'em. From Ambler, from Deighton, Greene, LeCarre, Ludlum. Sort of in alpha-

betical order. And Martin Cruz Smith. I just mix 'em up. A little of
one, a little of another. The unexpected confrontation, the switcheroo,
and, voilà—soon to be a major motion picture."

I could not imagine Joanna Gravesend getting hooked up with
Flaherty. She was not a literary groupie. As a matter of fact, I can't
recall her ever mentioning a book in my presence. Hard to recall her
ever mentioning *anything* in my presence. I'd never talked to Joanna
alone. I was always with Sally, who led me away quickly after she and
Joanna had exchanged smiles and pecks on the cheek. It pleases me to
believe that Sally was being possessive. Or defensive.

But Joanna was one of those cool, slender brunettes with delicately
plucked eyebrows and shiny hair who stare stonily at you out of ads in
The New Yorker, swathed in mink and leaning on a Bentley. And she
was just as real to me as the women in those ads.

Alden Crowley wouldn't tell me anything. Flaherty was a sort of
enigma. I was still stuck in my swivel chair wondering where to start,
when Reiko appeared in my door. She looked bemused.

"There are a couple of guys here to see you. I asked them what it
was about, and did they have an appointment. They just stood there
deadpan and asked to talk to *you.* Any reason the FBI might be lookin'
for you?"

Well, now, I had worked on a number of cases that involved
government contracts with Silicon Valley companies. Could be one of
Washington's bureaus might have heard of me. I tried to remember
the most recent jobs I'd had tripping through the chips in Cupertino.

"Let 'em come in, honey. I'm clean. I *think.*"

The two men who entered my office wore dark suits, white shirts,
and plain navy blue ties. If they had been younger, I'd have taken
them for a pair of Mormon missionaries. They stepped in front of my
desk and stood silent. I rose to my full five feet eleven and a half inches
and greeted them with what I have always imagined to be a cordial,
ingenuous smile.

"Gentlemen, what can I do for you?"

"Mr. Riordan, I am Conrad Schneider and this is my colleague, Earl
Stramm. We're with Omicron Megabyte Systems. You did an investigative job for us a while back involving industrial espionage, remember?"

Schneider was the taller of the two men, and a shade older than his companion, ramrod stiff and painfully formal. Stramm, on the other hand, was baggy and slouchy, and obviously bored. His idle gaze took in my office, lingering on my always out of date day-at-a-time calendar, and an ugly bowling trophy which had been left behind by a previous tenant.

I remembered the deal with Omicron Megabyte (a name changed to protect *me*). OMS, as I learned to call it, is a small outfit in Monterey working in artificial intelligence and voice-response technology. I had helped them turn up a mole who was happily stashing yen in a Swiss bank account as the result of feeding information to clients across the Pacific.

Schneider went on: "We have another problem, Mr. Riordan. Our CEO, Mr. Arthur Wilson, who you may remember is a close friend of Mr. George Spelvin, who recommended you to us in the first place, has been made aware that a group of investors in San Jose is planning a takeover move against us. We're not really sure who the people are. That's why we're here."

Stramm, the rumpled one, seemed to emerge from his brief trance. He spoke, in a whimsical, lazy voice:

"We think we know a couple of the guys, Riordan. They live around here and know about us. But the muscle—the money—is in San Jose. And, believe me, we're not in a hell of a good position to fight them. We went public just over a year ago. We are sitting ducks."

"Who are the local people?"

"A stockbroker named Carlos Vesper and one of his clients, an investor whose name is Highbridge. Vesper has a kind of shady rep. Highbridge just has a lot of money."

"Isn't Vesper the guy everybody's suing?"

Schneider answered. "The man has a long history of litigation, and has always emerged without stain from the courtroom. That's what worries us most. Vesper is very, very dangerous. As a manipulator, that is."

"How are things with Arthur Wilson? How's the new technology coming?"

The men exchanged glances. Schneider spoke: "Well, it's hard to tell. We ... we're not really into the technical side. We're ... administrators."

I thanked the gentlemen for thinking of me, told them I was really quite busy at the moment, but that I would gladly look into their problem as soon as possible. At my usual rates, of course.

That seemed to satisfy them for the moment, and they left. I yelled to Reiko.

She appeared in my door, eyes blazing.

"Don't yell at me, turkey. All you need to do is walk ten feet to the door—if you can get your lazy ass up off that chair. Or you could use the intercom thing on the telephone."

"The goddam intercom thing on the phone costs too much money *because* you *are* only ten feet away, and we don't need the bloody thing. Sit down."

She took her time sitting down, tilting her nose in the air, and carefully smoothing her skirt with the air of Elizabeth II.

"I need you to undertake an outside job. As I've told you, your friend Howard Gravesend's wife is divorcing him. Howard, of course, is guilty of all kinds of adultery. But he needs to protect himself in the settlement, and he wants me to get the scoop on his wife, who, he thinks, has been sleeping around. Get the picture?"

She deigned to nod.

"Joanna knows me. I can't follow her or stake her out. I'm good, but that's too big a handicap. I want you to handle the investigation of Mrs. Gravesend. You've already hinted that she isn't exactly the long-suffering faithful wife."

She snorted, but said nothing.

"I don't really have to suggest this, I know, but you might enlist the help of your wide-spread, well-informed family. They seem to know everything. Or, at least, how to find out about everything."

She stared at me for about a minute, her eyes the narrowest slits, and fingered a large enameled Japanese character she wore suspended on a gold chain around her neck.

"I will do your bidding, all-powerful one, on one condition."

"What condition? What do you mean 'condition'?" I was a little angry.

She squared herself around in the chair and planted her elbows on my desk. Her hands became tight little fists.

"I have worked for you for more than ten years. I came to work cheap because I thought you needed me. Besides, at the time, I didn't need the money. By and large, we've had a pretty good relationship. I've done a lot of your legwork and you've been good to me. But now there's got to be a change. I want to be your *partner* now. I want *Riordan and Masuda* on the door!"

"OK," I said, surrendering to the inevitable.

Reiko got up, walked around my desk, and planted a wet kiss on my widening bald spot. She was skipping as she left the room.

4

"The end is the grave, the grave is the end. The poor bastard."

I DON'T KNOW that I really intended to do that—make Reiko a full partner. *And* part of the firm name. But I do know that she was absolutely right in what she said.

If Reiko had not come along when she did, I'd probably be supporting a small headstone in Colma, San Francisco's City of the Dead. She saved me from the ravages of strong drink and self-pity. She put me back in the world after Helen died. And she has been an important part of my life ever since.

When she left my office, I contemplated having the inscription on the door changed. "Riordan and Masuda, Private Investigators" sounds pretty dull. A company name in this racket needs some pizzazz. What the hell. I'll think about it tomorrow.

But I didn't have a chance to "think about it tomorrow."

I unfolded the copy of The Herald that I had laid on my desk earlier and was faced with a grinning portrait of Howard Gravesend, who, according to the story, had somehow during the previous night "met with a bizarre accident." His body had been found, skull fractured, against the stone fence at the base of the Tor House tower. Time of death, according to the coroner, had been fixed at about 3 A.M., and it was gently hinted (in semi-polite journalese) that it was believed that Gravesend had consumed more than a trace amount of alcohol.

Howard and Joanna had lived most of their married life in a relatively small house (for Carmel Point) on Stewart Way, just a hundred yards or so from Tor House. I don't think that Howard had ever heard of Robinson Jeffers, much less read the man's poetry. Joanna, though, was a member of the Tor House support group, where she must have met Michael Flaherty. Howard may never have read anything but legal reference tomes, but he most certainly had heard of Flaherty. And the author presented just the sort of glamorous facade that Howard knew was attractive to his wife.

The paper didn't come right out and say it, but the clear implication was that Howard was thoroughly drunk, that he wandered out into the night, felt inspired to climb the tower—and fell off, breaking his crown most grievously. An underworld figure whom I consult now and then has told me the sound is not unlike that of striking a cantaloupe with a ball peen hammer.

Well, that certainly sounded like a conclusion to the Gravesend case. Joanna wouldn't need her divorce. The legacy from the mysterious uncle in the West Indies would probably go to her, and that would be that.

It's tough to admit it, but one of my first thoughts was about my commitment to Reiko. If she didn't have to check out Joanna, would I still have to make her a partner? Well, hell yes, it was about time.

I called the Sheriff's office and asked for Sergeant Tony Balestreri.

"I'm sorry, Sergeant Balestreri is on vacation. Could someone else help you?"

"Vacation? He never takes a vacation. Says he's going to wait until all his kids are out on their own."

"They made him do it, Mr. Riordan. The told him *everybody* has to take a vacation. Practically pushed him out the door. He said he was going to rent a large recreational vehicle and tour the eleven western states. It sleeps eight, he said."

"Who's on the Gravesend case? You know, the guy who went off the Tor House tower."

"I'll check." I heard the click of the hold button, and listened to forty-five seconds of "I'll Be Seeing You" (probably now in the public domain, very popular during World War II).

The operator came back on the line.

"Sergeant Paul Edwards has been assigned to the case. But they tell me there's nothing to it. A drunk fell off a high place and smashed his head against a stone fence."

"Thank you, Thelma. Is Edwards around?"

I had known Paul Edwards longer than I had known Tony Balestreri, but we'd never been very close. Paul is a big black man who played basketball at Cal Berkeley, has a masters in philosophy, and sings show tunes in various entertainment spots around the Peninsula.

A good many years ago, a client of mine going through a very painful divorce proceeding was arrested by Edwards for being drunk and disorderly (not to mention abusive) at the Highlands Inn. When Paul Edwards showed up at the request of the hotel management, he pinioned my client with one great arm, and walked him slowly to the familiar white car with the green stripe. I walked along beside the two men, pleading for my client's release into my custody.

"*You* were the one he hit. Why do you want to take care of him?" asked Edwards.

"I've been doing a job for him, Deputy. And it was just a glancing blow."

"What were you doing for him?"

"I'm a private investigator. When I showed him evidence that his wife was cheating on him, he blew up. He swung at me."

"In ancient Greece, the bearer of bad news to the king often lost his head. Don't blame him. *You* guys are the carrion birds. I'm taking him in. For his own good."

"You don't understand. He made a habit of beating up his wife. She was just looking for some affection."

Edwards stopped and glared at me. "Are you *for* him or *against* him?"

"I don't like him, but he hired me and I have to protect him."

The officer pushed my client at me roughly. By this time, the man was limp, and it took all my strength to support him.

"Take the sonofabitch, investigator. But don't let me hear of any more ruckus from him."

Paul Edwards is a lot of man. Our paths have crossed occasionally in the years since that first meeting, but not since I had moved down from San Francisco.

When the deputy came on the line, he wasn't especially cordial.

"Riordan? I heard you moved to Monterey. Tony Balestreri bailed you out a couple of times since you've been here, right? Tony's too kind, you know."

"Paul, it's nice talking to you. Congratulations on making sergeant."

"What's your interest in Gravesend?"

"He was a client. Just another divorce case. I talked to him just the day before he died. He was in good spirits. I know he drank a good deal—no pun intended—but . . . climbing the tower at Tor House and falling off in the middle of the night sounds like a bit much to me."

"I'm sorry, Riordan. What we found was a guy with a badly fractured skull at the base of the tower. There was blood on the stone fence. We figure he sort of swan dived. Bang! Busted head. Case closed."

"Any other marks on the body, Sergeant?"

"Call Phil Marshall at the morgue. As far as I am concerned, it was accidental death. Keep in touch, investigator."

Marshall was an old acquaintance also. He was the M.E. on my first Carmel murder case, which involved a young female artist found dead in her cottage at the Old Ranch, a sort of resort motel. An abrasive bastard, but he was smart and thoroughgoing.

"Oh, yeah, Riordan. The case of the naked lady with blood all over her at the Ranch. How've you been, sport?"

"Doctor, you have at hand an ex-client of mine who evidently did a header off the tower at Tor House through a loss of equilibrium induced by booze. Correct?"

"Gravesend? God, what a name. Name like that, a guy doesn't have a chance, does he? The end is the grave, the grave is the end. The poor bastard."

"I understand it's the name of the little town in England the family came from, Doctor. But no matter. Have you got a full report yet?"

"What's to report? Dead by severe insult to the brain as the consequence of a humungous skull fracture."

"Could it have been caused by other means than the fall?"

"Hell, yes, somebody could have dropped an anvil on his head. But there's no blunt instrument pattern, if that's what you're after."

"How about the autopsy?"

"Over and done with. Aside from overweight and a very fatty liver, the deceased had been in good health. And hung like a horse, I might add. You'd be surprised how many big, macho guys with tattoos that come in here have such little bitty. . . . "

"Never mind, Doctor. Thanks for your help. I may call you again."

"Wait a minute, Riordan. There's one thing that might interest you. The guy's blood alcohol level was over point-one-oh, y'know. But not that much over. And a man that size with a drinking history can usually navigate. But, shit, what do I know?"

I thanked the medical examiner and hung up. I wondered how Robinson Jeffers would have felt about a drunk falling to his death from the tower the poet built himself.

It was late on an August afternoon. The sun was bright outside, having finally burned off the summer fog around two o'clock. It was an ideal time for a walk on Carmel Beach. Which is what I was doing when I started telling this story.

5

"I liked the man in a way.
But he was an ass."

I WENT DOWN the stairs to Alvarado Street and walked around the corner to Bonifacio where my car was parked in a twenty-five minute zone. There was the usual citation from the meter maid tucked under the wiper on the driver's side. I removed it and stuck it in my pocket. I write these things off as one of the costs of doing business and the IRS hasn't complained yet. I usually pay them in groups of five or six, especially the ones I get in Monterey. The authorities are getting pretty testy about parking tickets. Just shortly after the Pope's visit to the Peninsula, the Parking Commission was providing the cops with lists of offenders with five or more outstanding tickets, and threatening to immobilize their cars with the dreaded "Denver Boot." The fact that they could only afford five "Boots" sort of diluted the threat. But I hate the thought of finding my beloved Mercedes two-seater, grimy and oxidized as it is, strangulated by such an insidious device.

You've got a fair shot to find a place to park on a weekday in summer in late afternoon at the foot of Ocean Avenue in Carmel. I got there just as a VW Rabbit cabriolet with the license plate RAGIBUN was vacating a space very close to the beach.

21

My custom, when it comes to a beach walk, is to start at the foot of
Ocean, walk north to Pebble Beach, then back south to Carmel Point
before returning to my car.

A friend of mine, a golf nut, told me once that this was the best way
to get to the Crosby Pro-Am Golf Tournament (when it was Bing's
own clambake). You parked in Carmel and walked up the beach to the
golf course. He never told me just when the tournament officials began
intercepting the beachwalkers and charging them the proper fee. But I
hate golf and he knows it. The pursuit of the little white (or orange or
yellow) ball around the countryside strikes me as about as stimulating
as watching game shows on TV back to back. But I must be in the
minority on the Monterey Peninsula, where there might be enough
golf courses to accomodate the entire population simultaneously. And
during a drought these playgrounds soak up about half the water
available to North Monterey County.

I opened the car door and sat sideways to change to my desert boots.
I love to walk the beach, but I can't stand sand in my shoes. I took off
my coat and put on a windbreaker against a pretty stiff ocean breeze,
and grabbed a shapeless cotton hat that Reiko bought me at Banana
Republic to match a hat of her own. I keep it in the car to avoid the
destruction of the exposed area of my monk's tonsure from the ravages
of the sun, and to protect what's left of my hair.

Even in the coldest summer weather there are those who take
advantage of the few hours of sun we get some July and August days in
Carmel. There are slender young women and wiry young men who
must drop whatever they are doing when the sun appears, slip into
their bikinis and dash to the beach. On days when the smell of wood
smoke is heavy and fireplaces are glowing all over town, the sun need
only appear for an hour to lure these people to its rays.

I plodded along the beach considering that thong bikinis the size of
three eye-patches could (or *should*) be worn only by very young
women with perfect figures. I saw none of such description that day on
the beach. The sunbathers find stretches of flat sand behind high
dunes that protect them from the wind. Along the water's edge during
these sunny hours, there's always a string of small children, screaming
and splashing, watched closely by anxious mothers wearing tight head
kerchiefs and heavy jackets. In the cold water are optimistic surfers in

androgynous wet-suits, making the most of the tentative waves that roll politely up to the white sand of Carmel Beach.

When I chose to walk no further north, I turned and looked at the view. In the earliest Carmel days of Jeffers this was very different. No luxurious homes along the ocean front, no teen-age kids pumping loud rock music out of jeep-type vehicles, no surfers. No, it was pristine white beach as far as the rocks of Carmel Point, maybe somebody galloping a horse along the water. In the hazy distance beyond the nearer land projection of the Point, was the tip of Point Lobos. A few trees, not nearly the woodsy look of now. The live oaks, the cypresses, the pines—most were planted here where there had been only grass and scrub.

The poet walked the beach for inspiration, to evoke the muse, as it were. Since muse-evoking ain't exactly on my agenda, I walk the beach to clear my head. It also helps to burn up a few of the excess calories I am inclined to take in on any given day. I *could* say that I am certainly not a poet. But who can say which of us is a poet when so many of us never try to write a poem? I'll have to check with Sally about that. She's got a Ph.D. in something or other, I forget what.

A voice from behind me:

"Riordan, is it not?"

I turned to see the shaggy figure of Michael Flaherty. The collar of his tweed jacket was turned up, and a woolen muffler trailed in the breeze. In contrast, his faded jeans were rolled to mid-calf, and his feet were bare.

"Hi," I said. "Come here often?"

Flaherty haw-hawed loudly and slapped his hand on my shoulder.

"Every day, my friend, every goddam day. You know how it is with writers. We need solitude. I find it on the beach. Most days."

"You're not really a poet, are you, Mike? I've been thinking about Jeffers."

The "famous author" air disappeared and an expression of quiet reflection took its place.

"Oh, God, Riordan, how I wish I could write like that man. I've tried, you know. But nothing happens. I make quite a show of reading his work aloud for groups. Well, you've heard me."

We stopped, and he looked out at the sea.

"I write exciting, convoluted melodramas about places I've never been. I've lived here for thirty years. I saw *him* here. I saw the poet walk the beach. But I can't write poetry—not a line. I can describe in detail a chase through the Casbah in Marrakech. But I always have to worry about somebody writing my trusting publisher and telling him that there *isn't* any Casbah in Marrakech. You don't know, do you?" He seemed pretty anxious. "I can describe a pitched battle in Afghanistan. But I have to imagine the terrain and the weapons, and I've made some awful blunders. Thank God, most of my readers don't notice. But poetry. . . . "

There was a faraway look in his eyes. I figured it was time to change the subject. After all, Howard Gravesend had suggested that Flaherty might have been carrying on with the beautiful Joanna—and now Gravesend was dead from a fall off the poet's tower. The Sheriff had labeled it "accidental death", but after what the medical examiner told me, I wasn't at all sure. And, although I knew that there wouldn't be any money in it, I was inclined to pursue the matter.

"You heard what happened at Tor House?" I asked.

Flaherty snapped out of his reverie quickly.

"Poor Howard. Yes. What a strange way to go. Especially for a man who had no use for poetry whatsoever. Bizarre. I wouldn't put it in a book and, hell, I'll use *anything*."

We walked on ten or fifteen paces.

"Y'know, Michael, that Joanna was suing him for divorce." I watched him out of the corner of my eye. There was no special reaction.

"Yes, she told me."

Well, that was up front. She told him.

"Howard hired me to get the dirt on *her*."

"I'm not surprised. I liked the man in a way. But he was an ass."

I decided to press further. "He even suggested that you and Joanna might be more than friends." That was pretty coy for me.

Flaherty threw his big head back and roared his big "haw-haw." "He was absolutely right, old man. Joanna and I have been lovers for more than a year. Best lay on the Peninsula, by God." He winked at me and grinned through his beard. "Now that little admission will throw some fat in the fire, won't it, Pat. How's this: I wanted Howard out of the way, invited him up for a drink, bashed his head in, then dragged him over the wall into the Tor House garden, hauled him up to the tower, and threw him off. No, wait a minute. I'd have to get him dead drunk, *then* drag him up to the tower, and make sure he went off head first into the stone fence so that he'd break his skull. But why the tower? There are so many more convenient ways to get rid of some-body around here. How's about having the body turn up on the race course at Laguna Seca. They're setting up the stuff for the Pope's visit next month. *Or*—oh, Lord, the inspiration—the firing ranges at Fort Ord. The body—barely identifiable—discovered after a nighttime exercise. . . . "

His eyes were afire, but he was laughing at me now. He broke into a trot and headed for the stairway up to Scenic Road at the foot of Eleventh Avenue, waving as he went, his laughter loud and clear in the salt air.

6

". . . Lt. Col. Edward Summers, retired, of Carmel."

M EANWHILE, back at the office: When I walked in next morning, I could see that Reiko was fuming. She sat rigid at her computer, and the anger radiated in all directions. She's a sweet girl, really, a kind soul who rescues stray animals and feeds unsalted peanuts to the scrub jays, birds of little charm and raucous sound.

"What's eating you, Reiko-san?" I asked, projecting as much innocence as possible.

"Screwed again, Riordan." She didn't look at me. "Screwed again without being kissed. You promise me a partnership if I undertake to get the goods on Joanna Gravesend. I get the job done. Then that bastard husband of hers gets himself killed, and lets her off the hook."

"Wait a minute, honey. Maybe this thing isn't over yet."

"What do you mean, not over? You've got no client. You didn't even get a retainer from the loudmouth bastard. He got drunk and killed himself falling off that tower. So Joanna was sleeping with four or five guys. So who cares?"

"Four or five guys? Hey, Michael Flaherty told me yesterday that *he* and Joanna had been lovers for more than a year."

"On alternate Tuesdays, maybe. I *told* you. Before you ever gave me the assignment. The lady was fond of sexual intercourse. Now, that isn't bad, of course. But she chose some strange partners."

I know that a lot of people would accuse me of being sexist if I called Reiko just about the "best Girl Friday a man ever had." Come to think of it, the term is pretty demeaning. Come to think of it, I can't remember *what* day it was when she appeared in the doorway of my ratty San Francisco office and decided to adopt me. But it was love at first sight, although my eyes were pretty bloodshot and my brain was pretty cloudy.

"You're my partner, Reiko-san. Your name goes on the door." I figured maybe in smaller letters. You can't destroy a man's ego *altogether*. "Tell me what you know. I'll figure a way to make some money out of it."

She brightened up instantly, popping up from her chair to begin the little dance she does when she's excited.

"When I started asking around—checking my relatives, like you said—the first name that came up was Alden Crowley, the law partner. I thought, that's too obvious. Besides, he's filing her divorce suit."

"I know that, partner. So far, old stuff."

"Hold on, will you? Everybody knew about Flaherty, the writer. He *told* everybody. And she didn't seem to care. But he was just one of a group. The others were a real mixed bag. There's a very straight, uptight insurance agent who lives in Marina with a wife and four kids. There's a guard from Soledad Prison who's meaner than a junkyard dog. How about a sixty-four year old lettuce grower in Salinas who might be the wealthiest man in Monterey County?"

Reiko was very proud of herself. She stopped her little dance in the middle of the room, and faced me squarely with her hands on her hips.

"But lately, the guy she's been spending the most time with is Lt. Col. Edward Summers, retired, of Carmel. He lives in a little house on Torres Street by himself, and he may or may not be engaged in covert activities for the CIA."

It was interesting up to that point.

"You have been watching too much TV, my friend. I know that the trendy thing for retired military officers is to get into some sort of mercenary or espionage activity. In fiction, baby, fiction. I don't want this case to degenerate into material for one of Mike Flaherty's spy novels."

"You better believe it, *partner,*" she said, meaningfully. "Two of my cousins are civilian workers at the Presidio. I checked out Summers as soon as I learned about his connection with Joanna. He is forty-five years old, a bachelor all his life, retired four years ago with a lot of medals, including a Purple Heart with three clusters. Served three turns in Viet Nam. Drives a Corvette and paid cash for his house. Now, isn't *that* interesting?"

I have reached a point in life when I am surprised by very little. We who make a living asking embarrassing questions tend to get pretty jaded. But I still am not quite sure I understand the mysterious ways in which Reiko gathers information. It is as if her personal network of operatives works as a giant flesh-and-blood computer. All she has to do is enter a question, and in twenty-four hours she's got more answers than she knows what to do with. Reiko's family, anchored on the Monterey Peninsula in Pacific Grove by her Uncle Shiro (who owns the building that contains our office), is spread all over the Peninsula and throughout the San Francisco Bay Area. Most are professional people of all sorts, though there seems to be a disproportionate number of dentists. There are enough lawyers to go around. There is a curious case on the books in which Dennis Omi was the plaintiff's attorney, Frank Umemoto the defense attorney, and Dan Fukushima the defendant. They were all first cousins. The trial only lasted a half hour because Judge Harry Masuda disqualified himself as the defendant's uncle. The fact that he was also uncle to both attorneys didn't seem to bother him.

"So what else?" I asked with resignation.

"Well, Dave Gonzalez, who works for my Uncle Shiro, does Summers' gardening, and he has seen a regular *stream* of suspicious characters go in and out of the house, and . . ."

"Stop. Calls for conclusions on the part of the witness. I sustain my own objection." I react like this frequently, the result of having gone all the way through law school and flunking the bar exam. But that's another sad story.

She glowered. "There was a stream of suspicious characters in and out of the place. *And* Joanna Gravesend was there frequently, taking the sun on a little deck that comes out of the shade between two and three in the afternoon on days when the fog burns off. She would lie out there in her teeny bikini bottom and nothing else. Thought she couldn't be seen. But Dave doesn't miss anything."

"OK, so we've got Joanna hooked up to a lot of people, including this shady retired light colonel who entertains suspicious characters. So?"

"My cousin Harold—he's Shiro's oldest boy—is an accountant, a CPA. Two years ago, he was approached by a man who said he had formed a new company, and was looking for an accounting firm. Harold had just opened his own office and was eager. But when he asked the guy the nature of his business, he got smoke blown at him. 'Defense Unlimited' was the name of the firm. The man told Harold it was a sort of employment agency. My cousin got a little curious and told the man he'd get back to him. Harold found this ad in the paper a couple of days later. And he found out that the man who placed it— who had visited his office—was Lt. Col. Ed Summers, USA, retired."

She handed me a raggedly torn piece of newspaper on which appeared an ad one-and-a-half columns wide and two inches deep. It read:

GENTLEMEN WANTED

For possibly hazardous work.
When applying, please list:
1. Age and appearance (including photo)
2. Education
3. Current and past employment
4. Availability
5. Languages

Please forward to: Defense Unlimited and
indicate mailing address.

The ad included a P.O.Box number, Carmel, CA 93921, the zip of the downtown post office where all Carmel citizens and business people must go to get their mail.

I was a beardless PFC in Korea, and I don't want to study war no

more. Lt. Col. Summers' ad clearly implied something like a mercenary recruitment program. Not that this sort of thing is unusual now-
adays. Not from *my* generation. I carried a rifle and froze my ass, saw a
buddy blown to hamburger a few feet away. But it seems that, despite
the bitterness and resentment of a lot of Viet Nam vets, others didn't
get enough excitement, or figured it was on-the-job training. And there
are always the macho types who didn't see any action, or were too
young, who think that combat is like you see it in some movies: lots of
shooting, but only the bad guys get hit. These are the clowns who are
out in the woods shooting yellow paint at each other. I say send 'em all
to the Middle East and let the young guys come home.

"Summers is training troops in Central America, operating a task
force in South Africa, infiltrating Iraq with Egyptians, or Egypt with
Iraqis. But nobody speaks the same language, and I don't know what
I'm talking about. Are your sure about this ex-colonel, Reiko-san?"

She grew indignant. "My cousin Harold is absolutely reliable. He's a
CPA, isn't he?"

I couldn't argue with that. The whole crazy story of Joanna's
involvement with Summers and Summers' involvement with God-
knows-what threw a lot of new light on the Gravesend affair. But it was
strobe light, and it didn't illuminate very much for very long.

7

"Remember what happened to Boesky."

REIKO SAT confidently in the uncomfortable chair I use for my clients and looked pleased with herself. Evidently she was waiting for some kind of answer. I tried to look judicioius.

"Now that we are partners, Reiko-san, we will have to share the load equally. However, this does not mean that I have to do billing and use that infernal machine you insist on having. And we can't afford to hire a third party just yet. Does that sound OK? Are you ready to live with that?"

I spoke slowly and deliberately, watching Reiko's face, which had grown sober and impassive. She spoke very slowly:

"You know I'll do any damn thing that needs to be done in the office, *partner*. I suspect you're laying the groundwork for some sort of con. You're thinkin' my name on the door will be smaller than yours, right? Forget it. Or was it something else?"

The lady knows me too well, I thought. And yet I try to patronize her too often. I sighed.

"Remember the guys who looked like federal agents who were in here the other day? They need my professional assistance. They are not G-men. The case is one of industrial intrigue, an area in which I have the expertise. There's good money in it. I would like you to take over the Gravesend case and see what you can get out of it. Surely there's somebody involved who'd be willing to pay an investigator."

Now, I didn't really want to dump the most interesting case to turn up in Carmel since Sheila Lord bled to death at the Old Ranch. But the office needed revenue, you know what I mean? And in my heart, I knew that Reiko could find a way to make a buck out of the Gravesend affair.

"OK." She brought her small hand down sharply on my desk with a resounding smack. "I will follow up every lead on the death of Howard Gravesend while you do whatever it is you're going to do. Just be sure you keep track of expenses."

She rose, tugged down her skirt, and strode out of my office. Reiko is wearing minis these days, as well she might. Good legs for a small girl. This is all stream-of-consciousness stuff, you understand.

I called to her as she went through the door: "One more thing, kid. Try to find out why the guy died at Tor House. Symbolism and all that. I've got this nagging feeling about poetic justice. There's a lot of gloom and doom in Jeffers' poetry. It doesn't seem to connect with a clown like Howard Gravesend. But there might be something there. Got it?"

"Sure, *partner,* I thought of that, too. It's my case now, remember?"

So, for a while we were going our separate ways. As a matter of fact, it was several days before I saw her again.

I had promised to look into the impending hostile takeover of Omicron Megabyte Systems of Monterey. The name invoked by the two blue-suits who came to my office that day was Arthur Wilson, a close friend of my great benefactor, George Spelvin. I should explain to you that I do not use George's real name in this or any other narrative in order to protect his aristocratic heritage. George is pretty flakey, but he's done a lot for me.

However, Arthur Wilson was another matter. Unlike George, who never worked a lick in his life, Wilson was a self-made man, a brilliant electronics engineer, who actually used money he *earned* to buy his house in Pebble Beach. I had met him socially a couple of times at George's place, and I had worked with him briefly on the case of industrial espionage I have already told you about. I admired Wilson very much.

I drove out to the Omicron plant on Garden Road near the airport. Start with the fundamentals, I always say. Don't get cute until the fat lady sings, to coin a phrase.

Wilson received me warmly. He's a man who can be terribly busy, doing two or three things at once, and yet seem to focus on whomever he's talking to. But he has a sneaky way of curtailing an interview gently and kindly, and you never realize you've been curtailed until much later.

"I'll lay it out for you, Pat. I took this little business public a couple of years ago and it has done reasonably well. It wasn't a big issue and it sold out in a hurry. Moved up by fractions and has grown to this day. Well, the business is solid. We've developed some advanced technology that, I think, IBM has no idea of yet. As you might know, I started this business just to keep my hand in. I made all the money I'll ever need with my first company. But Omicron is my baby, and I don't want to lose it.

"What I want you to do is to find out for sure who's organizing this takeover. We're pretty much convinced that Carlos Vesper is behind it. But Vesper is a fraud who has barely kept his ass out of jail. He personally owns twenty-five shares of Omicron, the minimum purchase at issue. With two-hundred and fifty bucks invested, he is somehow—we think—trying to manipulate the stockholders. Vesper has no money of his own. There are others—in San Jose—who are behind him. Pat, I'm prepared to offer to buy back all the shares at a premium—if I have to. It closed at twelve and a half yesterday, and I'll offer fifteen, no questions asked. But, for God's sake, don't tell anybody that or it'll shoot the shares up. And don't *you* go out and buy Omicron. Remember what happened to Boesky."

With my resources, I was not about to dabble in the stock market. It took only a few seconds of figuring in my head to determine that at twelve and a half bucks a share, I could afford maybe twenty shares. I put aside the idea of selling Reiko's computer rig mainly because it wasn't—isn't—paid for yet. Anyhow, she'd kill me.

As he gave me the tongue-in-cheek warning about insider trading, Wilson had me by the elbow and was steering me out of the austere, uncarpeted office that was hardly bigger than mine.

"Keep me posted, Pat. Call Schneider or Stramm if you need help—

or money. One's a yuppie jerk and the other's a slob, but they are *very* good at what they do. They complement each other pretty well, don't they?"

As I left Wilson's office, I couldn't help thinking that he was the only rich person I knew that I could talk to without feeling uncomfortable. Here was a man just a few years older than I am, enormously successful, who worked every day in a small office when he wasn't out in the plant or the research and development lab, had lunch at his desk except on rare occasions, and who wore a button-down blue oxford cloth shirt tieless, with faded jeans and running shoes. My kind of guy. Except much, much richer. Well, *some* of the very rich are not much different from you and me, despite what Scott Fitzgerald said.

8

"You needn't have made such a fuss, Riordan."

I DIDN'T KNOW a hell of a lot about Carlos Vesper. Except, of course, what I'd read in the papers. The man was a slippery character, no doubt. But I figured he must have had some kind of charm or people wouldn't have trusted him to such a degree that he could lose all their money while making a lot for himself.

Before I could confront Vesper—if that was what I had to do—I needed to learn as much as I could about him. So I checked out my sources, official and otherwise, on the Peninsula. This is the composite that emerged: Vesper was youngish, early thirties. Very young to have earned such a questionable reputation. He lived well, had a house on Forest Knoll in the Skyline Forest area of Monterey, drove a Lamborghini Countach. The man dressed well, probably in a style that he imagined a Wall Street tycoon might affect. He was seen at many social gatherings and accepted in many prominent households, despite the dark cloud that hovered over him. Handsome, a skillful charmer.

"A real doll," said Sally Morse over lunch at Kiewel's. She had come over to Monterey from her Carmel office on Ocean Avenue, ostensibly to have her hair done, but really hungry for my company, a fact which I patiently explained to her. "Could charm the pants off any woman of

any age. Maybe literally, although he doesn't have *that* kind of reputation. Just a pleasant person to have around. Single, good-looking, well-
mannered, intelligent. I set up some European trips for him. Alone.
South of France, Zurich. Always alone. Good-looking young guy with
a lot of money, but alone. I wondered about that."

"No girl friends?"

"Oh, sure. Lots. But I can't remember seeing him with any girl
twice. That *is* odd, isn't it?"

"I dunno, Sally. Love 'em and leave 'em, maybe. In character
analysis, sexual orientation or activity is, I think, much overrated. Jesus,
I sound like a guest expert on 'Donahue'. Is there anybody you know
who is close to this guy? I mean really tight?"

"Funny you should ask. Joanna Gravesend knows him *pretty* well. I
watched her sneak out with him at a couple of parties. And hang all over
him at other very social events. She wasn't his date, you understand. Jo
and I have known each other a lot of years, but whenever I asked her
about Vesper, she'd just give me this wise little smile and clam up."

I am not at all surprised when I become aware that one case I am
working on has even the remotest connection with another. The
Monterey Peninsula is my prime turf, and despite the growth of the
past couple of decades, it's pretty small. And since the people I work
with mostly come as the result of my connection with George Spelvin,
they tend to belong to a certain group: old families, rich families, and
climbers. Come to think of it, never has there appeared in my office a
pitiful, penniless waif, pleading for my help.

"What's the best way to approach Joanna? I mean, to ask her about
Vesper."

"Straight ahead, man. Don't try to sneak up on her or she'll cut you
off right now. Call her up, ask her what you want to know, and see
what happens."

Kiewel's is in a complex of buildings overlooking Fisherman's
Wharf that started out to be a sort of shopping center but has been
taken over in large measure by offices. The restaurant is fairly new and
has a certain popularity among the locals, especially military person-
nel from the Presidio. I, for one, hope it stays around a while. Eating
places on the Peninsula seem to come and go with depressing regular-
ity. Kiewel's has a wonderful view of Monterey Bay and a deck that is

delightful on warm, sunny days. Of course, there are a lot of days when the fog and the breeze can chill a casserole in under two minutes. But we Peninsulans tend to ignore the elements most of the time.

I walked Sally to her car, and sent her on her way. She had driven both of us to the restaurant, and I had to walk back to the office, a not inconsiderable distance. During my walk I practiced in my mind effective approaches to Joanna Gravesend.

Reiko was not at her desk when I arrived at the office. A note was taped to my inner office door: "Partner, pls note. I am engaged in researching the activities of Lt. Col. Summers, USA, ret. This may take a while. Guess you took a long lunch. We'll have to talk about that. Messages on the machine. Your partner."

I hit the button on the answering device. There were the usual hangups, some of them noisy and frustrated, but there was an efficient-sounding female voice asking if I could call Mr. Crowley's office.

Which I did. When Alden Crowley came on the line, he was disturbed.

"Riordan, goddamit, what's going on? This little Japanese girl bounced into my office this morning claiming to be your partner and asking all sorts of questions about Howard and Joanna. Got pretty goddam personal! I'd like an explanation, if you have one."

I had to think fast. I couldn't disclaim Reiko. If it got back to her, she'd come after me with her treasured samurai sword. But I didn't want to alienate Crowley, so I wedged in a small apology. "She's just doing a job, Alden. We've been retained to investigate the circumstances of Howard's death." I lied. So far as I knew, nobody was about to pay us for work on the Gravesend case.

That really didn't satisfy him, but it seemed to placate him for the moment. He knew enough about confidentiality not to ask about my fictitious client.

"Be careful, Riordan. And keep the little Jap off my back. Understand?"

That really pissed me off.

"Alden, if *ever* again you refer to Reiko as 'that little Jap,' I promise you I'll come over there and break your face. Do you understand?"

"Easy, Riordan. No offense. Just an old reflex. You and I were, what? Ten or eleven during World War II. Sorry."

"Hate to tell you, Alden, but you're older than I am. Call me if you have any further complaints. But I might not answer." I hung up.

It burns me when I hear some upscale professional WASP like Alden Crowley use an ethnic slur. But I guess there's still a lot of that stuff around.

I just sat around for a while, turning over the known facts about the Omicron case in my mind. Arthur Wilson was an honorable man ("... so are they all, all honorable men"). Omicron was kind of a hobby to him—he said. He had made his fortune years before, creating a whole new direction for electronics in his garage in what was then the quiet little California town of Sunnyvale. Only one small fact disturbed me. If Omicron had only been a hobby, an adventure to keep Wilson busy, why the hell did he take it public in the first place? Why didn't he just keep it his own private toy?

"Hello, Riordan."

I knew the voice. There was no mistaking the throaty tones of Joanna Gravesend. I had been rotating slowly in my swivel chair with my eyes closed when she spoke. She could have been there for several minutes or just have walked through the door. I jumped to my feet, sweeping the phone off my desk and, with incredible reflexes for a fellow my age, caught the instrument inches from the floor, dropping to my knees with considerable impact and accompanying pain. As I tried to rise, a corner of the desk caught my right temple, stunning me for a matter of seconds, and my swivel chair leaned majestically backward in slow motion, finally crashing noisily to the floor.

"You needn't have made such a fuss, Riordan." The lady glittered as she stood there, not because of the ring she wore, whose blue-white solitaire diamond looked like it should be weighed in ounces rather than carats, but rather because her *presence* was sleek and shiny, as if she had been reproduced in full color on that heavy coated paper they use in fashion magazines. "I just dropped in for a chat."

"Please sit down, Joanna." I was hyperventilating just a bit while righting my chair with as much dignity as I could muster.

"Well, now," I said, settling in with a fixed smile on my face and beads of perspiration on my upper lip. "A chat, you say. What about?"

She inspected the chair thoroughly, flicking off crumbs from Reiko's morning brioche. ("I always use your desk if I'm messy. You'd never notice," says my partner.) Joanna carefully arranged her skirt as she sat. She fixed me with an unblinking stare.

"I know that Howard came to you before he died and asked you to investigate me. I know that you and your little friend have been asking questions about me. I have come here to set the record straight."

Joanna was not especially beautiful this close up. Her nose is a bit too long, her mouth a bit too wide, and her eyes a millimeter or two too close together. But she has acquired skills over a lifetime of forty-odd years that enable her to conceal the flaws, and she is indeed a knockout. What she looks like when she gets up in the morning is another matter.

"Well . . . straighten away, Joanna, straighten away."

She took a pack of cigarettes from her purse (Virginia Slims, by God, I *knew* it!) and made a brief questioning gesture for my permission. I don't smoke (or drink, or wear a Chicago fedora), and I don't like cigarette stink in my office, but what could I say? With the same fixed, toothy smile, I nodded briefly. She lit her cigarette with a tiny gold lighter and blew smoke in my face.

"Howard hired you to investigate me. You know I filed for divorce. But the day after Howard hired you, he was killed. You probably think I had something to do with his death. I didn't. He probably told you about his uncle's will. That was bullshit. No uncle, no will, no fortune. What he really wanted was something that belonged to me. He figured to use you to blackmail it out of me before I could divorce him." She looked around briefly, and tapped her ashes on the floor. I pretended not to notice.

"I will admit that I have not been sufficiently circumspect in my relationships with men other than my husband. It wouldn't be hard to prove a case for adultery against me. But Howard lost interest in me early in our marriage. We haven't been living together for nearly a year. Howard bought the house in Carmel Meadows for me, but he's been living in the old cottage on the Point. And for the sake of my own needs—and maybe my self-esteem—I turned elsewhere."

"Joanna, you mentioned that Howard was trying to beat you out of something that belongs to you. That intrigues me. What is it?"

She took a deep drag on her cigarette and blew the smoke in my face again. I got up and opened the window. There was a pretty good breeze from Alvarado Street, and it did immediate damage to Joanna's coiffure. But she didn't seem to notice.

"It's a manuscript that's been in my family since my great grand-father acquired it over a hundred years ago. A collection of poems in the author's own hand. Never published. Worth a fortune. With an inscription to my great grandfather on the first page: 'For my dear friend, Hamilton Manning from Robert Louis Stevenson.'"

9

"These guys are coming to get me."

OF COURSE I have read all of Stevenson's great adventure novels. Of course I knew he had chased a married lady to Monterey in 1879, stayed a few months and took off. The brevity of this sojourn and the spiciness of it don't seem to matter to the natives. The fanciest private school in the area is named after Stevenson. It is, of course, in Pebble Beach.

But poetry? When I was a kid, I read A *Child's Garden of Verses,* as any properly raised child should. But that was it, I thought, in the poetry department. *Treasure Island* and *Kidnapped* were staples of my youth. I consider myself fairly literate, but I was unaware of any poetry for adults in Stevenson's oeuvre. But it could explain something about Howard Gravesend's fall from Jeffers' tower. Maybe Howard just got the wrong poet.

We both sat in silence for a minute or two. I finally thought of something to say: "Joanna, I don't need to know this stuff. Why did you come here, anyhow?"

"I did a foolish thing, Riordan. I was concerned about the manuscript when Howard found out about it. It was one of those little things I hadn't bothered to tell him about when we were married. I kept it in a safe deposit box in my name only. Lately, though, I became con-

cerned that Howard might somehow get hold of the key—he could
fake his way into any bank vault, y'know—so I took the manuscript out
of the box and gave it to a friend for safekeeping. He's an ex-
soldier ... "

"Lt. Col. Ed Summers, the mystery man of Torres Street." It wasn't
hard to call that one. Nor was it a shock to Joanna that I called it. "So,
again, why do you come to me?"

"Ed hasn't been at his house since Howard's death. His car is gone.
Ordinarily he would have left me a note—but ... nothing. That's why
I'm here, Riordan. I want to hire you to find Ed Summers—and the
manuscript."

Well, now, *finally* a paying client in the Gravesend affair. I would
never have believed it could be Joanna.

"Have you told Crowley about this business? He's your lawyer."

"No. I mean, yes, he's my lawyer. No, I haven't told him. Alden and
I *did* have a brief fling years ago, as you probably know. But, now he's
just helping me with a legal matter—or *was*. He filed my divorce
action. But I don't really trust him. He wasn't much as a lover. And
men like that aren't really trustworthy, are they?"

I didn't know how to answer that question, so I ignored it.

"Any idea where Summers might have gone?"

"None. He was always disappearing for a week or two at a time. I'd
go to his place—I have a key—and there'd be a note about his being
called out of town on urgent business. Then, after a while, he'd be
back. I'd ask him where he'd been, and he'd put on a face like G.
Gordon Liddy and quietly tell me to go to hell. Now that I think of it,
he *looks* like G. Gordon Liddy."

"Does he know the significance of the manuscript? How valuable it
is?"

"I don't think so. He never reads anything but *Soldier of Fortune*
magazine."

"Do you know who he hangs out with? Other than yourself, of
course. Any cronies, business associates that you know of?"

"Nobody, Riordan. I met the man at the bar in the Pine Inn in
Carmel. He picked me up, if you really want to know. That was in
March, I think, four or five months ago. We've been on a regular, uh,
schedule ever since. More or less."

I thanked Mrs. Gravesend and ushered her out the door, promising to keep in close touch about the matter. She gave me a friendly peck on the cheek in the hallway, and left a trail of stale cigarette smoke and expensive perfume in the stairwell.

I was in a quandary. Reiko was presumably working on the Gravesend case, and, in particular, the activities of Lt. Col. Summers. But I hadn't seen her, and I didn't know where she was. Joanna Gravesend had been in my office and I hadn't thought to ask her about Carlos Vesper. I had to get on with Arthur Wilson's investigation into the mounting threat against his company.

I left a note on Reiko's desk: "Please hold still long enough for a conference. Urgent. Very truly yours."

It was time for me to get into motion on Vesper.

The easiest way to get from my office to the Skyline Forest where Vesper lived is a roundabout way. My office is on Alvarado Street, the "main street" of Monterey, even though the next parallel street to the west is called Calle Principal, which *means* "main street."

I headed out Pacific to Highway One and up the hill to catch Highway 68, the "Holman Highway", past the hospital to the Skyline Forest gate. This is to me about the most thoroughly livable part of Monterey. It's woodsy, the streets run in all directions, many ending in cul-de-sacs, and a lot of them provide ocean views. Of course, Skyline Forest gets a lot of fog, as does the neighboring town of Pacific Grove. But, my friend, if you choose—as I do—to live on the Monterey Peninsula, you learn to love the fog. When it's 110 degrees in Sacramento—or Omaha or Chicago or Philadelphia—the heat weave has probably raised the temperature to an unbearable 75 in Monterey.

When I pulled up in front of Vesper's house on Forest Knoll, I saw a dark-haired man in faded jeans and a sweatshirt illustrated with a portrait of Johann Sebastian Bach, urgently cramming things into the cargo space of a Ford station wagon. I wondered what had happened to the Lamborghini Countach. It wasn't hard to recognize Vesper from his newspaper pictures, even without a drink in his hand. I pulled into the driveway.

"Hey, what the hell do you think you're doing? You're blocking my drive, and I'm leaving in a few minutes. If you're selling something, I don't want any. Now, get out of my way." He continued to stuff

various things into the wagon while he shouted at me. I deliberately
went into slow motion as I got out of my car, and approached the man
in what I believed to be the rolling gait of John Wayne.

"Mr. Vesper?"

He eyed me suspicously, with just a hint of panic.

"I do not bear a subpoena, Mr. Vesper. I merely came to ask a few
mild, unincriminating questions. And I'm not going to move my car
until you answer them."

He seemed to relax just a bit. His body sagged and he dropped an
expensive leather case to the ground.

"Who are you?"

"My name is Riordan. I am a private investigator in the employ of a
gentleman who thinks you have designs on his business."

"Wilson," he said in a strangulated tone. "Wilson hired you because
he thinks I'm trying to put together a grab for Omicron. I'm trying to
get out of town before some other guys get here to kill or maim me.
And you want to ask questions." He sighed. "Go ahead. Ask."

"Why are these guys coming to kill or maim you?" That wasn't the
question I originally intended to ask, but it seemed like a good one.

"I don't know what you know about me. I'm a stockbroker. I've
worked for the biggest in the business and have done very well for
myself. But I wasn't very happy. So I went to work for an outfit in New
Jersey that specializes in 'growth companies.' It was an easy sell. Cheap
stocks, lots of blue sky, very little growth. I made a great deal of money
in a matter of months by conning widows and retired people. And the
Peninsula is full of them." He sat on the right front fender of my
Mercedes and folded his arms.

"Then I heard something about Wilson's company. It was on the
verge of a real breakthrough in the electronics industry. Of course,
breakthroughs are an every day occurrence in that business. But this
one was supposed to be dynamite. And the stock, which sold at ten
dollars in the initial offering, hadn't hit ten-fifty yet. And I heard
something else. Arthur Wilson, one of the original shirtsleeves guys in
computers, was almost broke. He could be had. His company could be
had. I went up to Silicon Valley and lined up the cash. And it looked
like a sure thing. Still does."

"So why are you running? I'm not clear on that."

"Goddamit, I told you. These guys are coming to get me. If you know *anything* about me, you know I'm being sued from all sides. By the people I sold those 'growth' stocks to. But this one guy—who called *me*, I didn't call *him*—doesn't want to wait for a court. He wants satisfaction now. He's a retired army officer who lives in Carmel . . . "

"And his name is Lt. Col. Edward Summers."

Vesper's face went pale and his jaw dropped. "You know this guy. You *work* for him?" He began to back away from me, looking around, I guess, for a rock or a stick to fend me off with.

"Remain cool, man. I do not work for Col. Summers. I merely know him as a mystery man who is involved in too goddam much of my business. What you said about Wilson being almost broke. Elaborate on that."

"What I heard was that Wilson had started Omicron as a big toy to play with. But then some of his investments began to go sour, then others, then something like a disaster. He *had* to go public with Omicron to raise money. I got all this from a guy who belongs to a literary group with me."

"A literary group?"

"You surprised? Sure, we're all writers—or would like to be. I write blank verse, myself. My friend is into haiku. You see, pal, you can't make a living writing poetry or novels. There's only about a dozen big ones who make important money, aside from convicts, football players, super-patriots, show biz freaks, and unfrocked politicians. What did you say your name was?"

"Riordan. I don't write. I paint. Dogs. Paintings of dogs. Not that the paintings *are* dogs. They're pretty good, really."

Vesper was smiling for the first time. He's a good-looking, rather charming fellow, and I could see how a lot of people would buy snake-oil from him. But we had got somewhat off the subject.

"So you think Summers has a couple of guys coming to break your legs. Where do you think you can hide?"

"San Francisco. I can disappear there. I've done it before."

"OK. I don't want you to be crippled for life. I'll move my car—on one condition: Tell me where you can be reached. And if you try to fake me out, I'll find you and *I'll* break your legs."

He gave me a telephone number. I've made quite a study of area codes and telephone prefixes. Gives me something to do during those long hours I spend in the office waiting for business. "This is for real? The numbers *sound* right, but ... "

"It's a woman I know. She's a cellist with the symphony. I was attracted by her great knees. Female cellists always show their knees. Ever notice that?"

I filed that bit of intelligence away for future use, moved my car, and waved him on his way.

10

"Welcome, rojin-san," she said . . ."

WHAT I HAD HERE, I thought, was a funny mess of fish. And Lt. Col. Summers provided a common element, a sort of missing link. The sonofabitch could have killed—or arranged the death of—Howard Gravesend. He was a somewhat dissatisfied customer of Carlos Vesper. And he had the Stevenson manuscript. I wondered if the bastard wrote poetry. I was running into more would-be poets and failed poets in an investigation that started with a divorce and a nonexistent inheritance. Poor old Howard died in a fall from a tower built by a poet, and now the chase was on for the missing poems of one of the great writers of the nineteenth century. A veritable gathering of poets.

I was pretty sure Arthur Wilson didn't write poetry. I hadn't yet met a successful Silicon Valley entrepreneur who professed an interest in poetry. Oh, they claimed that their machines—properly programmed—could write poetry. The damned things could play chess, couldn't they? That certainly takes more brains than writing poetry, they'd say. I don't know about that. I once stood for an hour on the sidewalk in front of an Ocean Avenue game store in Carmel, watching a computerized chess game playing itself. I called every move twenty or thirty seconds before the machine made it. And I'm a lousy chess player. Sally Morse's ten-year-old nephew beats the hell out of me every time.

But poetry is something else. For some reason, I have always had a special feeling for poetry, even though the only collection in the house during my early childhood was *Heap o' Livin'*, by Edgar A. Guest. As I grew older, I began to get more sophisticated as well as more romantic. Of course, I had to conceal these feelings from the other members of the football team. There's a guy in my racket who has a reputation for spouting poetry for all occasions. He even has the name of an Elizabethan poet, although I suspect that he changed one letter for effect. He operates out of Boston. Maybe I ought to start up a correspondence with him.

It was a brilliant summer day. I watched from the dead end of Forest Knoll as Vesper's station wagon disappeared up the hill. From my car I could see, between two handsome, well-cared-for houses, a magnificent view of Monterey Bay. Around the Peninsula folks pay premium prices for a view like this. I have trouble understanding that. Where I live—a little house in Carmel that belongs to George Spelvin—I can't see the ocean or the bay, or much of anything else. But if I get out of the house and walk for five minutes I can take in the entire length of Ocean Avenue to the beach and get for nothing a vista that the folks on Scenic Road have paid an extra couple of hundred grand for. And if I don't like dodging surf boards and listening to loud rock music (Is *loud rock music* a redundancy?), I can walk for five minutes and be home. I pretty much stay off Ocean Avenue in the summertime, though. I have to fight this awful urge to walk up to some tourist in short shorts and a tank top, grab him by the shoulder straps and say,"What do you think this is, fella, a bloody beach resort?" I guess it really *is*, but it didn't start out to be. These people who figure they're on vacation in California so it's time to take their clothes off are all staring at me in my hooded running suit. When they get home, they'll tell the neighbors they had a hell of a swell time time but, jeeze, was it cold in Carmel! Here's a picture of me and Angela in front of the Hog's Breath restaurant, but Clint wasn't there.

I headed the car downtown. It was late in the afternoon and I figured I just might catch Reiko in the office.

Usually a parking spot on my block of Alvarado opens up magically when I approach the office but this time, no soap. I wound up in the covered public parking facility on Calle Principal, found a meter with time left on it, and walked down the passage to Alvarado that emerges right across from my building.

"Welcome, rojin-san," she said, with a grin that was almost obscene. It was what I learned in the infantry to call a "shit-eatin' grin," although I was never sure of the connection. Also, "rojin-san" is a Japanese address of great respect that made me cringe. Roughly, it means "old person with dignity." "Reiko," on the other hand, means "spectacular girl-child." I was sure she had a lot to tell me.

I thought I'd better control the conversation. "Before you begin, let me tell you that there have been some pretty interesting developments. We now have a real live paying client on the Gravesend case."

"I know. Joanna Gravesend. She called a half-hour ago. Wants you to call her back."

"There are *other things*." I was irritated. Reiko always seems to be about half a step ahead of me. "Things seem to be getting more complicated on the Omicron thing. You'll have trouble believing this, but Carlos Vesper is hiding out because he believes Lt. Col. Summers has strong-arm guys after him. Vesper also says Arthur Wilson is in financial straits. But Wilson told me Omicron was just a hobby. And Summers has disappeared with a rare manuscript . . . " I couldn't believe what I was saying.

Reiko just sat there grinning at me and playing with the Disneyland back-scratcher she keeps on her desk for God knows what reason. "Go on," she said, "I know about the Stevenson manuscript. Joanna told me. We got real chummy on the phone."

Shaking my head, I went into my office and collapsed in my chair. Reiko followed and stood nearby, scratching her back with obvious relish (*and* the Mickey Mouse back-scratcher). She noticed the look of wonderment on my face. "Oh, I do this all the time. When you're gone."

I told her painstakingly of all my activities of the past two days and related the information I had accumulated. She was particularly intrigued by the interest in poetry of so many of the figures in these two cases.

"I really don't think Summers is a poetry freak," she said. "He might have a collection of dirty limericks. But it isn't likely he's a fan of T. S. Eliot. Or even Dr. Seuss. I think I know where he is, though."

11

"There isn't any," she said.

I T MAY NOT be necessary, but I'm going to tell you anyhow that I am in love with Reiko, and have been ever since she took over my office a year after my wife died. She is a mighty mouse, standing a full five feet in Reeboks, with shiny black hair cut short in what we used to call a "page boy," and the face of an oriental doll. And she's smarter than I am. Well, just as smart. Let's just say she'll match me when she gets more years on her. And I'm in love with her. In a particular way, you understand. There's a twenty-year gap between us, and, being of the old school, I could never see romancing such a young one. Some of my friends are convinced that I have had an affair with Reiko. Not true. My generation is bracketed by the Roaring Twenties and the Era of Sexual Freedom, and we never got in on any of the fun. I think I would have married her if I'd had half a chance. But Sally Morse is closer to my age, and if I've got to sin, she suits me fine.

Reiko went into her office and came back dragging her tatami mat, a gift I had presented to her as a token of affection and a souvenir of a pretty fascinating murder case. Call it a cultural consciousness or something in the genes, but Reiko insists she can think better on her tatami mat. She knelt down and rocked back to sit on her heels. I've tried it, but I can't manage the pose for more than ten minutes. Reiko can remain in her mat position for hours.

When she left me the other day, she said, she had gone straight to Alden Crowley's office, thereby giving rise to Crowley's indignant phone call to me. When she realized that Crowley wasn't going to tell her a damned thing, she left, bowing with eyes downcast, and backing out of the office with tiny geisha steps.

"The asshole was insulting," she said. "I did my Shirley Maclaine bit. You know, where she had to play a Japanese in that real old picture."

" 'My Geisha.' Early sixties. With Yves Montand. You must have been about ten years old. How . . . ?"

"I rented all of Shirley's pictures on tape. When she started pushing reincarnation. I had to find out how she got that way. The pictures didn't help. She seemed so normal." Reiko looked disappointed. But she continued her report.

"I figured the most interesting guy in the whole mish-mash is this retired Lt. Col. Summers. So I staked him out. I took my camera and parked near his house. And watched."

Reiko's ten-year-old Mustang is in no better shape than my car. It couldn't attract any curiosity parked on a narrow Carmel street. I'm convinced that everybody in town has at least one junker just used to negotiate the blind, unmarked intersections. You know that sooner or later your're going to get creamed, so why waste money or risk having your insurance cancelled.

She had driven up to Torres Street and found a spot from which she could observe the Colonel's house. It wasn't long before she got some action. She described the procession of characters who visited the place:

"Nobody stayed more than fifteen minutes. They were all men. I didn't recognize any of 'em. They were sure a tough-looking bunch. All in civilian clothes, but they *looked* like soldiers, know what I mean? Well, they kept arriving and leaving, like on a schedule for a couple of hours, and then—this'll shake you up—who should arrive but Arthur Wilson." She sat back with a very smug look.

I just looked dumb. "You're sure it was Wilson?"

"Positive. I've seen the man's picture thirty or forty times. Couldn't miss. He drove right by me and I was near enough to touch him. Dark grey Continental limo, the kind you'd expect a chauffeur to drive. And, get this, he drove right into Summers' garage. Activated the door opener and drove right in. By the way, I've got pictures of all this."

"How long did he stay?"

"I'm not sure. After about an hour, Summers came out carrying a big suitcase, with both hands on the handle, and had an attaché case tucked under his arm. He loaded the suitcase—it must have been really heavy—into one of those Japanese jeep things—I've got a picture of this, too—and drove away. I had to make a quick decision. I decided to follow Summers. God, what a trip!"

She told me the whole story:

She had followed Summers carefully. She was inexperienced at tailing people. But Summers appeared to be inexperienced at being tailed. He never looked back.

Summers drove up Torres to Ocean and straight up the hill to Highway One, with Reiko following along. The Colonel turned south at the Highway into a long line of stop-and-go traffic down the hill. Soon it became clear that he was going to make the left turn into the Carmel Valley Road, a tricky move on a good day, but dangerous on a midsummer afternoon. Summers made his turn, and Reiko watched as the northbound traffic cut her off. She was able to follow in ten or fifteen seconds, though. Summers was no more than a couple of hundred yards ahead of her.

He didn't seem to be in a hurry. He was cruising along at about forty on the straightaways, and Reiko had no trouble settling in behind him at a safe distance.

Summers slowed down through Carmel Valley Village, but didn't seem inclined to stop. Reiko, who had never been beyond this point in the Valley before, began to feel a little nervous, but, with a firm grip on the wheel and a comforting glance at the gas gauge, she clamped her jaw and kept an eye on the car ahead.

The Carmel Valley Road runs through a range of hills along a system of creeks until it joins Arroyo Seco Road which loops north to connect with U.S. 101 near Soledad, a town whose name means "solitude," and whose points of interest include a mission and a prison.

But Summers turned west on Arroyo Seco and Reiko almost lost him. She followed the jeep for another few minutes until he slowed to turn into a parking area of a picnic ground.

She slid her Mustang into a slot a good distance from the Summers vehicle. As she watched, the Colonel alighted, carrying the attaché case he'd had tucked under his arm back at the house. He walked briskly into the picnic area, and headed for a group of men at a table far from the parking lot.

Reiko had to keep her distance. A small Japanese in a camouflage jump suit and a floppy Banana Republic hat stood out in a place like this, chiefly occupied by harassed parents and screaming children. She stayed fifty yards from Summers and his friends. But she was still able to verify that at least two of them were visitors at Summers' house earlier in the day.

In a few minutes, two of the men came back to the jeep and got the huge suitcase Summers had brought. Reiko had watched the Colonel load it in the vehicle without too much difficulty. But the two men seemed to be having trouble and carried it back to the table as if it were a steamer trunk.

As they neared the group, the man in front stumbled and sprawled, sending his end of the case to the ground with a jolt. Even at her distance, Reiko could see the cold, threatening look on Summers' face. He said something to the man, and it obviously wasn't, "I trust you're all right, Charlie."

The men lifted the case to the table and stood around it, cutting off Reiko's view. One of them appeared to open the case, there was a brief conference around the table, and another man closed it. Then the meeting adjourned abruptly. Another pair of men bore the suitcase to a pickup at the far end of the parking lot. Summers returned to his jeep. Reiko walked briskly back to her car. She waited for Summers to clear the lot, and she took up the chase once more.

This time it was a simple reverse. Reiko followed Summers back the same route, pausing half a block away as he pulled into his driveway. The Colonel got out with his attaché case in hand, and went into the house.

"I didn't know quite what to do at this point." Reiko rocked back and forth on the tatami mat. "Obviously I couldn't follow Summers into the house. And I was *very* curious about Arthur Wilson because I didn't see him leave. Was he still there? Or had he left when I was chasing Summers to the Arroyo Seco picnic grounds?"

She decided to hang around. In a half-hour or so, Summers came out of the house, got in the jeep and, in an obviously practiced move, backed out of his driveway in a tight arc and stopped. The garage door swung up and out came the dark gray Continental with Arthur Wilson at the wheel. The electronics genius headed down Tenth Avenue and turned north on Junipero. Reiko continued to watch the house as Summers drove his vehicle into the garage and closed the door.

"Wilson lives in Pebble Beach. He was probably going home," I said. "We don't know how long he was in Summers' house. He could have been in and out several times while you were away. What he was *doing* with Summers, I have no idea. Unless—maybe he is behind Summers' threats against Carlos Vesper."

Reiko continued to rock back and forth on the mat. Her eyes were closed and her brows knit tight in an intense concentration that was beginning to give *me* a headache. I have a running argument with her about the value of a computer in the real world. Obviously, it's a losing battle, considering the many dollars we have tied up in the tentacled monster she has on her desk. I know I could never get her to see the point, but the brain under that shiny black hair is as good as any mess of silicon chips. There was no way that she could feed the information we had into her computer to get answers. The machine recognizes no nuances, cannot understand *human* nature. But Reiko can.

"Are you getting ready to channel some deductive genius like, say, M. Dupin?" "Channeling" is something she is into currently (the Shirley MacLaine influence).

"No, goddamit, I am using a perfectly natural mathematical process: finding the common denominator. Shit!"

She opened her eyes abruptly. She shook her head slowly from side to side.

"There isn't any," she said.

12

"Go away," she suggested.

BUT THERE WAS. And she found it. But I'm getting ahead of myself.

Reiko and I commiserated with each other for a short while, locked up the office, and called it a day.

It occurred to me as I got in my car that I hadn't seen Sally for nearly a week. I figured she must be missing me, so I parked in my driveway at Sixth and Santa Rita and walked down into the late summer tourist crowd in Carmel-by-the-Sea.

The walk down Sixth from Santa Rita to Junipero is exhilarating; the walk back up can kill you. There may be a few steeper hills in town, but this is *my* hill. I keep telling myself it's great for the old cardiovascular system.

Sally's office is on the second floor of the Doud Arcade. When I opened the door she was on the phone, evidently in a heated discussion.

"For God's sake, Kevin, I'm doing all I can. Sure, I live here. Sure, I know everybody. But this is a big thing. They're coming from all over. They're driving me *nuts!*"

Now, one thing about Ms. Morse that is constant—no matter what—is her grooming. Except on this occasion. Her hair looked like she had been running her fingers through it. Her lipstick was chewed off, and her mascara was staining her cheeks. Her jacket hung on the back of her chair, and her blouse was pulled out of her skirt. She had kicked off her shoes and was rubbing her left calf with her right foot. On the left leg of her pantyhose was a runner an inch wide and widening, running from ankle to modesty forbids.

"Call me in the morning. About ten." She hung up the phone and glared at me. "Go away," she suggested.

"But, Sally, I am frustrated. I need love and affection."

"You'll get none from me this night, Riordan. Go away. Or get me a vodka on the rocks. A double. But you don't drink, do you, you sanctimonious bastard."

"Hush, lady. I live only to do your bidding."

I went down the stairs to the cocktail lounge and bought a heavy vodka with a twist for her and a Clausthaler for me. These new non-alcoholic malt drinks are great for us teetotalling converts with a lingering taste for beer.

When I got back to her office, Sally looked like herself once again. She had had the opportunity to comb her hair and repair her make-up, and she was nearly calm. She had discovered the run in her hose, and she had her skirt hiked up to examine the damage. She plucked disconsolately at the threads, muttering small obscenities under her breath.

I put the drink down on her desk and sat down to admire her excellent legs. In a moment, convinced that the situation was hopeless and aware that I was ogling her thighs, she tugged her skirt down with an indignant jerk, and wheeled around to the desk. She lifted the vodka glass to her lips with a little sigh, and drained half of it in a gulp.

"What seems to be the trouble, madam?" I asked in my most professional manner. "Obviously, you are disturbed. I suspect that you were affected by having to compete with your mother for your father's love. Or that you suffer from long term damage arising out of sibling rivalry. Or perhaps were molested by a maladjusted uncle."

"Sometimes, Riordan, you can be a horse's ass. That may even be unfair to the horse. My mother and father were and still are devoted, and I adore them both. I have only one sibling, a brother who lives in San Jose, and my only uncle is a priest. But you know all that.

However, in your own idiot way, you got a message from my telephone conversation. I was talking to my uncle. He teaches at the University of Louisville. He and about a million others are trying to get here for the visit of the Pope. They've been bugging me for weeks, everybody in the travel business across the country, old acquaintances I haven't heard from for years. Travel arrangements aren't that hard. They can always get into San Francisco. The big tourist season's over in mid-September. But after that it gets sticky. All the motels and hotels on the Peninsula are requiring a three-day minimum. And the seventeenth is on a Thursday. A week before Rosh Hashanah, believe it or not. First the Pope, then Jewish New Years. And, in between, Clint is entertaining some kind of European royalty, for God's sake. *L'chaim!*"

She swallowed the rest of the vodka and noisily chewed up the ice.

I am usually pretty much aware of what is going on in the world. The Herald is thrown somewhere near my house most mornings, occasionally before I leave for the office. I pick up the San Francisco Chronicle now and then. I watch the eleven o'clock news most nights. But up to that conversation with Sally, I had taken little notice of the visit of the Pope.

I *had* heard that he was going to say a mass at Laguna Seca. There was a lot of talk about the Diocese of Monterey charging twenty-five bucks a head for admission. And I vaguely remembered something about the beatification of Father Junipero Serra, the priest who established the California missions, whose body is buried in the Mission San Carlos Borromeo del Rio Carmelo, more familiarly referred to as Carmel Mission. The Pope was scheduled to visit the mission on his whirlwind day trip to the Peninsula. As I thought about these things, a little warning light began to blink in the back of my mind and I made a mental note to check with the Carmel Police.

"I understand your problem, dear lady. Let me take you away from this hassle for an evening of wining and dining, and, perhaps, a bit of passion."

"I can't go anywhere fancy with this godawful run in my hose." She pouted, rather fetchingly.

"I refuse to take you to McDonald's or Wendy's or Burger King." Nobility, as I have often said, is a terrible burden to bear. I patronize all those places frequently, dedicated as I am to the consumption of saturated fats. But for Sally, nothing but the best. "How about a bottle of wine and a nice plate of pasta at Paolina's downstairs?"

"It's August! The place is full of tourists! With strollers. And they're all wearing what in their hearts they feel is appropriate for a summer vacation in a resort. Some of them even wear the stuff they buy here. Have you seen the T-shirt that guy across the street is selling showing Clint shaking hands with the Pope? God, Riordan, what is happening to Carmel?"

She drove me up to my house to pick up the Mercedes and I followed her out to a steak and rib joint on the road out to Sally's place in Carmel Valley. Sally, convinced that she couldn't look grubbier, scarfed up a full order of ribs with great enthusiasm, taking them up in her hands, causing a fine red spray to stain her already rumpled blouse. I almost forgot to eat, so fascinated was I with Sally's complete abandon.

We were in separate cars, so I tagged along behind her to her garden apartment in mid-Valley. Sheepishly, she excused herself to take a shower. I browsed through Ms. and Architectural Digest until she came out, glowing in an old chenille robe, disarmingly shy, to lead me into the bedroom.

13

Arthur Wilson lied to me.

It SEEMS THAT the older I get, the earlier I wake up in the morning. My eyes snapped open at quarter to six, and I couldn't have gone back to sleep if I tried. Sally was still serenely asleep, her tangled hair cascading over her forehead, lips parted, making little noises in her throat.

I swung my legs out of the bed, got up and padded to the bathroom. Was there ever a time in my life when I didn't have to pee first thing in the morning? I don't remember. I washed my face, standing naked at the basin. When I went back into the bedroom, Sally was awake and propped up on her elbows.

"You're getting thick in the middle, Riordan. Cut out the fried stuff. How's your cholesterol?"

I reached hastily for my shorts. To be nude in front of a woman— even one with whom I have been about as intimate as you can get— makes me nervous. I always feel somehow as if my manhood is being *evaluated.*

I mumbled something about needing a cup of coffee, and pulled on my pants. Barefoot on the kitchen vinyl, I put the teakettle on to boil and got out the coffee pot. Ever since she heard about people dying in fires started by coffee makers, she has chosen to make her coffee with a

simple conical top containing a filter over a glass pot. You heat the
water and pour it through. Even I can do it.

Sally came out of the bedroom tying the belt of her chenille robe.
She looked at me curiously.

"You seem preoccupied, Pat. What's on your mind?"

I *was* preoccupied. Somehow, Sally's problems with the Pope's visit
had disturbed me. I had an uneasy feeling that all the machinations
Reiko and I had been observing were somehow connected—with each
other. And maybe, by a long chance, with the visit of the Bishop of
Rome, the leader of the world's Catholics. But I decided not to tell
Sally all of it. Not now. Maybe never. . "Not much, Sal. It's Howard
Gravesend's death. The sheriff's people say accident; I'm inclined to
suspect murder. And I'm working on a deal for Joanna that I can't tell
you about just yet. Reiko is chasing around after a spooky retired Army
officer. Then there's Carlos Vesper—you know about him. And Arthur
Wilson. . . ."

"Hold it. Wait a minute. Art Wilson is a client. A very *good* client. A
respectable—not to mention wealthy—businessman. He couldn't be
involved in anything you'd be interested in."

"But he *hired* me, Sal. He hired me because he was afraid Vesper
was mounting a takeover of Omicron. But *I'm* afraid he might be
involved in something else. Although what it is, I have no idea."

I poured coffee into two brown mugs decorated with cartoons of a
disgusting fat cat Sally happens to like. She sipped hers and nodded in
approval.

"I'm glad I'm not in your business. As frustrating as it gets, my job
never confuses me as yours does you. And I like not being confused.
God, do you know what time it is? Why the hell am I out of bed?"

We took our coffee back to the bedroom and she sat on the bed
while I got dressed in silence. I hadn't brought a razor, and the one
Sally uses for her legs and underarms looked grungy. I figured I'd have
to stop at my house to shave before I could do anything else. I know a
couple of days' stubble is fashionable these days, but not on me.

I kissed Sally goodbye about seven. She responded so warmly I
found it very difficult to tear myself away. But, goddammit, duty
beckoned.

As a rule, when I drive back home from Sally's, I'll turn north on

Highway One to Ocean Avenue, thence down the hill to my place at Sixth and Santa Rita. But this Pope thing was heavy on my mind, so I cut over to Rio Road to take a pass at the Mission. It was foggy that morning, and traffic was light. I drove past the Mission Fields tract. The Little League ball park where the Pope's helicopter was supposed to land adjoins the playing fields of the Mission School.

I did a tight U-turn at the Mission, and pulled up into the parking lot. God, I thought, I feel for the Carmel Police. It is really their baby. You see, for some reason, the Mission and its grounds plus the ball field are within the jurisdiction of the Carmel Police, while the area behind the Mission, including Carmel Point, is in the county, the sheriff's jurisdiction. All the Pope action would be in Carmel.

I looked across Rio Road at the lower end of Mission Trails Park, a wooded ravine that runs almost three-quarters of a mile up the hill, a terrible place to secure. I tried to visualize the crowd that would gather here just to catch a glimpse of the Pope.

The police of Carmel are all good people. They maintain order in their town with grace and charm. But on a given evening, their most serious mission might be to arrange a tow for a car parked in a driveway, or quiet a row in a crowded restaurant, or silence a barking dog. The visit of the Pope would require all the manpower—and womanpower—they could muster. And maybe then some. I was sure the sheriff's people would be there. The event becomes their baby when the Pope's helicopter lifts off for Laguna Seca.

There was a time in Carmel when the police department consisted of one chief and one patrolman who took turns operating one car that had to be parked facing downhill or it couldn't be started. And it wasn't that long ago. Today the department is staffed with clean-cut, bright men and women who look formidable with guns on their hips, but function mainly as public relations people for a village full of strangers.

I had been visiting Carmel for nearly thirty years before I came here to live. The changes that have occurred in that time are probably as evident to me as they are to the long-time residents, if not moreso. It's kind of like watching a child grow up. When he's living with you, you don't notice the changes. But if you don't see him for months, or years, he's hard to recognize each time you meet.

Ocean Avenue, when I first saw it, on a foggy day in the late fifties, was, well, *quaint*. There was a string of little shops on either side of the street from Mission to Monte Verde, some more shops and restaurants and art galleries scattered along the side streets for a block or so—and that was it. There was one hotel in the business section of Ocean and there still is—the same one. Bed-and-breakfasts and a few small motels dotted the side streets.

Today the number of accommodations and restaurants has maybe quadrupled, maybe more. I haven't really counted. Shops have been upgraded—or downgraded, it depends on your point of view. There's a jazzy shopping plaza occupying most of a city block between Mission and Junipero. And some—too many—of the quaint old shops have given way to really ugly souvenir and junk stores. The American Way is to make a buck, isn't it?

One of the candidates in that famous mayoral election was a prominent junk store operator who, sensing inevitable defeat, nobly stepped down and instructed his eleven or twelve supporters to cast their votes for Clint. They did, and a lot of other folks did, too. Whereupon our storekeeper set about to capitalize on the popularity of the movie star to the extent that the new mayor asked him to cease and desist. Another newsworthy squabble in a town one mile square.

And now the Pope. I decided to take a run up to the police station at Fourth and Junipero and talk to some of the people I knew. But I had to go home first. I didn't want to upset a police lieutenant with my unkempt, unshaven appearance.

My place is, as I have said, just three short, near-vertical blocks off Junipero at the corner of Sixth and Santa Rita. The walk to the police station sounds like a breeze. Santa Rita to Junipero, three insignificant downhill blocks. Sixth to Fourth, a mere nothing—but all uphill. I was puffing as I mounted the steps up to the police department's front door. The police receptionist is also the dispatcher. From her position she can enjoy one of the best views in Carmel, looking out through glass doors toward the Valley and the foothills.

"Those stairs are the last straw, aren't they. Sorta adding insult to injury, right?" She was being friendly.

I got out a strangled chuckle and asked for Lieutenant Miller, whom I'd met years ago when he was a patrolman and I was getting into altercations in saloons. He's the reason I don't have a drunk and disorderly record in Carmel. When first we met I was threatening to break up a place on Dolores Street. John Miller quietly put me in his car and drove me back to my motel. He even dragged me up a flight of stairs, fished out my key, and laid me gently on the bed. I looked him up the next day to thank him, and we've kept in touch ever since.

"Hello, Pat, what's up with you?" The Lieutenant is a big-shouldered man whose dark hair is beginning to gray quite a bit on the sides. He shook my hand warmly and invited me into his office.

"I'm curious, John. About this Pope thing. This has got to be a load on you guys."

Miller shrugged. "It's a bitch. We've been sweating it for months and it's getting worse the nearer we get to September 17."

"You're going to have help, aren't you?"

"We're bringing in every warm body we can find who's willing to come. There'll be the Secret Service, of course. The sheriff's people will be on the perimeter. But I'm not going to sleep very well until the events are over at the Mission, and the man is lifted off in his chopper."

"Any rumors? Plots against the Pope and all that?"

"The usual. Threats. Crank stuff. Oh, and there's a real flimsy report that some sort of international group is out to cause some kind of mischief, although nobody knows what. And the Indians."

"The Indians?"

"There's a bunch that believe that Father Serra was cruel to the Indians. Or maybe desecrated their burying grounds. I'm really not clear on that. You going to the mass, Pat?"

"I'm not a Catholic. You expect all people with Irish names to be Catholic, don't you? Well, my grandfather, a very stubborn man, had a heated discussion with a priest about money years ago, vowed he'd leave the Church rather than have priests begging on his doorstep the rest of his life. He did. Became a Baptist. All of us expected him to call for the Catholic last rites when he was dying. But he didn't. The stubborn old bastard died a Baptist. My father was sort of a Methodist. I've been shopping around."

"Good luck. I'm a Presbyterian, myself. Or my wife is. I'm afraid I don't get to church very often. What's your interest in the Pope's visit?"

"I'm not sure, John. I've been working on a couple of cases involving some pretty interesting characters. You know anything about a retired lieutenant colonel named Ed Summers?"

"Now, that's a coincidence. Lives down on Torres? Neighbors have complained that the man is running a business. Too many visitors who don't look social, know what I mean? Another was sure the guy's got a stash of illegal weapons. Too much activity in the middle of the night and all that. We've checked Summers' place out a couple of times. Nothing there." The lieutenant frowned. "Something disturbing about the man, though. No visible means of support besides his army retirement. Which hardly could provide him with his life style. He lives well, Pat."

"Do something for me. If you get any more reports or complaints on Summers, give me a call. I'll buy you a cheap lunch."

I thanked the Lieutenant for his help, and walked out into the Carmel morning. The fog had burned off early, and the sunlight hurt my eyes. Despite the summertime traffic in Carmel, the air is remarkably clear and sweet. It's the prevailing ocean breeze that does it. There's a constant cleaning process going on that carries the junk in the air inland, and keeps the town air fairly pure. Now, if they could only iron out some of these hills. But, as I've said, that's what keeps the old folks spry: walking the hills.

There was one source I hadn't tried to tap yet for information on Ed Summers. I went back up to my house to call Al McManus, who maintains a very small office in Monterey for the FBI.

When he came on the line, I identified myself.

"Who?" he asked.

"Riordan. The private investigator. You and I and Tony Balestreri of the Sheriff's Department chased a guy with a load of drugs through the Monterey Aquarium."

There was a pause. "Oh, yeah, Riordan. How are you?"

"Very well, Al. I need to talk to you about a matter, and I don't think it's so good to do it on the phone. How about lunch?"

"Today?"

"Today."

"Let me look." There was some shuffling of papers. "OK. Abalonetti's at the Wharf. Eleven-thirty. That all right?"

"I'll see you there."

Not a waster of words, he hung up. McManus was like the lawyer in
The Canterbury Tales: he *seemed* busier than he was.

I picked up the Herald from my table in the dining alcove. Front
page was full of a lot of wire stories about goings on in the Middle
East. I guess we are never going to understand the Iranis or the Iraqis.
They're ready to blame America for everything from failed crops to
fallen arches. And they get so worked up about it.

An article on page three stopped me cold. "Murder Attempt on
Local Manufacturer" was the headline. The story went on to say that
"a gray Continental driven by Arthur Wilson, president of Omicron
Megabyte Systems, was fired on by two gunmen at close range as
Wilson drove into the parking lot at his plant. The suspects ran to their
car and proceeded out Garden to Highway 68, heading in the direction of Salinas. They were pursued by a security officer from the
Omicron plant, but he lost them on the highway. Fortunately, Wilson
was not injured, although several bullet holes were found in his car."

This couldn't have anything to do with the potential takeover of his
business, I thought. Those business manipulators who specialize in
that sort of thing don't use the expedient of knocking off the CEO. But
who would shoot at Arthur Wilson? And why?

I called Omicron. There was no difficulty getting through to Arthur.
He sounded cool as a cucumber.

"What do you know, Pat. Anything to report? I hear Vesper has
skipped. Does that mean anything?"

"How are *you*? Any reason why anybody wants to kill you? Oh, hell,
there must be a reason. Do you know what it might be?"

"I'm completely in the dark. I was coming in to work, turning in the
drive to the parking lot, when these two guys opened fire. I ducked and
hit the accelerator. It's a wonder I didn't crash into something."

"You sound like it was nothing. Just a mild annoyance."

"What do you expect? I've been shot at before. Didn't I ever tell you
I was an eighteen year old kid in a foxhole with the 106th Division
when it was overrun during the Battle of the Bulge? A green kid with a
green division. I was shot at from all sides, Pat. Not too many of us got
out of that mess."

"Somehow I didn't figure you for Army, Arthur. Especially combat
infantry. I was in Korea myself."

"Hell, Pat. So was I. I was a captain by then, running a rifle company. Caught a piece of shrapnel in my ass in that one."

We told a few war stories. I found out that Wilson's outfit was not far from mine, and we reminisced about some of the better whorehouses in Seoul. Then I slipped in the important question:

"Do you know a retired lieutenant colonel named Summers? Lives in Carmel. I understand he was something of a red hot in Viet Nam."

"Oh, sure, I know Ed Summers. He's a lot younger than I am. But we were in the Reserve together. I commanded a unit in San Jose. Summers was a non com then. Then he went regular army. OCS, Viet Nam, he went right up the ladder until he was passed over for the bird. He figured then it was time to get out. Why do you ask about him?"

"His name came up in a divorce case I've been working on."

Wilson chuckled. "I don't doubt it. Summers is quite a lady's man."

"Have you seen him recently, Arthur? I'd really like to get in touch."

"Oh, I haven't seen Summers for several months. He gets around, that guy."

Arthur Wilson lied to me. And I'd have to find out why.

"Thanks, Arthur."

"No problem. If you catch up with Summers, give him my best."

By the time I had finished my conversation with Wilson, it was ten after eleven. I had to push it a little to get to Fisherman's Wharf on time. I parked among the tourists in the big lot, and stuffed a couple of quarters in the meter.

Abalonetti's is out near the end of the Wharf. It's popular place that grew from a hot, cramped little dining room behind a fish market into a presentable restaurant. Quite frankly, I liked the old place better. Monterey Bay squid has always been the specialty of the house. Fixed a particular way, squid (please call it calamari) tastes like abalone, a shockingly expensive shellfish that is beloved of the sea otter. I think that's why they call the place Abalonetti's. It's not a real Italian name.

McManus was there when I arrived, sitting in a corner, surveying the room with his constantly darting eyes, while his fingers played with a fork. I slipped into a chair opposite him.

"Well, Riordan, what is so important that you could not discuss it on the phone?"

" 'Would not,' Al, not 'could not'. First question: What are you guys doing about the Pope?"

"You know damn well that's classified. I can only tell you we have plans. We've all had input and we're formatted."

McManus was more bureaucrat than crime fighter. He lapsed into what I call compu-talk frequently.

"OK. I respect your position. Now, second question: What do you know about a retired Lt. Col. Edward Summers?"

I watched his face closely. It seemed to me that the eyes darted just a little faster, and a tightness developed in the jaw. He was about to speak when the waitress arrived. We both ordered calamari—sauteed, not deep-fried—and decaffeinated coffee.

When she had gone, I looked again at McManus.

"Well? Are you going to tell me? About Summers?"

"Why do you want to know about . . . that man?"

"He's involved in a case I'm investigating. He's got something that belongs to a client of mine, and I can't find him."

McManus was playing with his fork with both hands, almost as if he were trying to bend it with his mind, like Uri Geller.

The FBI man spoke very slowly and deliberately: "I can tell you only that the man whose name you mentioned is under surveillance and has been for some time. It has been alleged that he is in the employ of a foreign power. Don't ask me any more questions."

That meant the complete elimination of conversation aside from, "Pass the salt." McManus and I really didn't have any common ground for small talk. He ate his squid with enthusiasm, and left me with the check. As he left the restaurant, I could almost see the ghost of J. Edgar Hoover hovering over him.

The bus boy came over and refilled my cup with regular instead of decaffeinated, and I didn't even care. My mind was racing through all the mental notes I'd made about Summers, all the things Reiko had reported.

The sea lions were barking. The tourists were tossing fish scraps, and the fat scamps who hang around the Wharf were putting on a show. I walked back to my car and discovered, to my surprise and joy that my parking meter was defective and hadn't moved a millimeter. I decided to leave the car where it was and walk up to the office.

14

"In her post-coital languor she becomes quite talkative."

R EIKO WAS NOT at her desk when I got to the office, but I heard her voice from beyond the partition, in the cramped cubicle that is my private domain. She was indeed taking the "partnership" seriously.

Sure enough, she was seated at my desk, leaning back in my chair, and probably would have had her feet up if she hadn't been wearing a tight miniskirt. Sitting across from her, puffing great clouds of fragrant smoke from a curved meerschaum pipe with an elaborately carved bowl, was Michael Flaherty.

"Well, it's about time, Riordan." Flaherty extended his hand without getting up. I winced slightly at the unnecessarily tight grip, an intimidating tactic often used by men who aren't quite sure of their own macho.

"Michael has been telling me about his poetry, Pat. Did you know he writes poetry?" Reiko seemed uncomfortable, as if she had been caught with her finger in the peanut butter. And the shaggy writer already had her calling him "Michael."

"Bad poetry, my dear. I have already told your, ah, partner here about my bad poetry. Here I am in the same glorious surroundings that inspired Jeffers and Stevenson, not to mention George Sterling, Jack London, Mary Austin, and others of passion or genius or both. Not to mention Steinbeck, who wrote poetic prose. I am able to eke out but a mere king's ransom for my trashy novels. But I am not fulfilled." The great mop of hair rippled gracefully as he shook his head.

"Why are you here, Michael?" I asked, taking care not to swing into the phony Irish sing-song affected by our visitor.

"I came to find out if you've made any progress in your search for the Stevenson manuscript."

That gave me a start. All that hush-hush stuff Joanna gave me about Stevenson's poetry was maybe just a lot of bullshit.

"What do *you* know about the Stevenson manuscript?"

"Oh, come on, now, Patrick. Joanna and I were—are—lovers, don't you know. In her post-coital languor she becomes very talkative. She sometimes chooses not to light a cigarette because she is trying to quit, she says. On one occasion, she told me of the manuscript. I immediately offered her a very large sum for it. When I phoned her recently, thinking to take unfair advantage of her widowhood with an offer she couldn't refuse, she confessed that she had entrusted the papers to a shifty retired military type who had flown the coop, so to speak. And she told me that you are on his trail. So—what's new?"

"Nothing's new. Summers—the soldier in question—is still missing and unaccounted for. But Reiko could have told you that."

"I *did*," she said, with indignation. "Michael, tell him I told you Summers was still gone. Didn't you believe me?"

Flaherty sighed. He reached into his pocket and withdrew a wooden kitchen match which he struck on the underside of the right leg of his jeans. He held the flame over the bowl of his meerschaum until it reached his fingers, puffing deeply all the while. "I thought something might have turned up." I had to admit that the blend he was smoking in that pipe had a wonderful aroma. I haven't smoked in twenty years, but the fragrance of pipe tobacco still turns me on. Can't take cigarettes in restaurants, though.

I was still standing awkwardly in my office since both chairs were occupied. Reiko showed no signs of moving. And I shifted from one foot to the other. "I'll keep you posted, Michael."

"Tell you what, Patrick. It appears that Joanna has retained you to find Summers and get that manuscript back. I will pay you an additional five thousand dollars when you've accomplished your mission—*providing* you can help convince Joanna to sell the poems to *me*."

"Sounds like a good deal. I—we've got a lot going right now, so I can't make any rash promises. But we'll be in touch."

Flaherty rose slowly to his feet, scattering sparks from the pipe on my bare wood floor. He crushed my hand again, blew a kiss to Reiko, and set the furniture atremble as he clomped out the door.

The chair was still warm when I sat down and faced Reiko across my desk.

"How long was he here?"

"Oh, about a half hour. Isn't he *something*? World famous—and he's so . . . *humble*. I can see why Joanna is mad about him."

I groaned. "He is not humble. He has an ego the size of Chicago. And Joanna isn't mad about him. Or, at least, any madder about him than she is about half a dozen other guys she likes to go to bed with."

Reiko pouted. "I *like* him. He's sexy. You're just jealous."

Well, maybe I was. Although Joanna Gravesend was not my cup of tea, a man just naturally envies another man who has the knack of stunning the women with his animal magnetism, whatever that is. I looked hard at Reiko, who seemed to have drifted away.

"What have you been doing?"

She woke up and grinned at me. "Research, partner, research. I got really curious about Arthur Wilson's connection with Summers. So I went to the library. Know what I found?" God knows I didn't know what she found. I bared my teeth as I shook my head. "Some guy wrote a biography of Arthur Wilson. You know, the inauspicious beginnings and illustrious career of a business tycoon. Probably sold four or five hundred copies, mostly to libraries."

"Go on, go on. What did you find out?"

"Well, Wilson was in World War II—I guess you know that. And he was in Korea. And he stayed in the Army Reserve until the early sixties, long after he built his first factory and made his first million." She got up and began her little dance, moving around the room and touching things as she spoke. "When he left the Reserve, he formed an organization of service people and ex-service people, called 'Patriots for Freedom.'" She stopped right in front of me and clapped her hands. "And one of the young men who helped him organize it was Sergeant Edward Summers."

I had never thought of Arthur Wilson as the type who could organize something that sounded so patently right-wing as "Patriots for Freedom." He had always seemed so laid back, so easy-going, with a clear straightforward look that put me at ease, with the warm hand on my shoulder as he ushered me out of his office. So Reiko's tale came as a shock. So—Wilson and Summers were closer than the computer genius was willing to admit. Much closer.

"So what do you think is going on, Riordan? Wilson visits Summers. Summers drives to the park on Arroyo Seco Road with a suitcase full of something for a meeting with some pretty tough-looking guys. What does it all add up to?"

I got up hastily and sat in my own chair. Things were flying though my brain, and I needed to kick back and put my feet on the desk. Two things came back to me with a rush: Carmel Police Lieutenant John Miller's mention of an "international group out to cause some kind of mischief," and FBI Agent Al McManus' word that Summers "is in the employ of a foreign power." I wondered if all these things hooked up, if Wilson and Summers were hatching a plot together, and if their D-day was the 17th of September.

15

I was beginning to sweat.

W HAT ABOUT poor old Howard Gravesend? I figure you might be curious by this time. It was his death that got me involved with all these people and events. He was cremated according to his will. At least, that's what his partner said. His ashes were turned over to Joanna, who placed them on a shelf in her broom closet. There were few mourners at the memorial service at the Church of the Wayfarer in Carmel. Howard was an only child, and his parents had long since departed this life. He had many acquaintances—he was the life of any party—but few friends. Reiko went to the church service, although she hadn't really liked the man. She felt, she told me, an obligation to a client. But I think she was just curious about who might show up.

"Joanna was there. With Alden Crowley. And about a dozen other people who looked bored. It was kinda sad, Riordan."

The strange connection between Joanna Gravesend, Arthur Wilson, Carlos Vesper, and Lt. Col. Edward Summers, USA, ret., had overshadowed Howard's sudden, messy death at the foot of Jeffers' tower. I began to wonder whether or not it was related, somehow. Aside from the fact that he was a client for a number of years, and that he took great joy in teasing Reiko when he came to our office, I knew little about the man.

For a few days after the visit of Michael Flaherty, nothing much happened. Reiko and I were both occupied with some routine investigative chores, boring but lucrative stuff for insurance companies and law firms. Reiko is an ace at slapping subpoenas on people. Nobody ever suspects that this five-foot, doll-like creature is about to serve papers. She'll just step in front of the victim with the writ clutched behind her back, flash an irresistible smile, and firmly place the document in an outstretched hand. Then she'll give the person a snappy military salute and a "thank you," and dance away.

One morning, when the phone wasn't ringing, nothing was happening, and I had run out of leads on the whereabouts of Colonel Summers, I asked Reiko, "What do we really know about Howard Gravesend?"

"He was a kind of a horse's ass," she said. "But a *naive* horse's ass, if that's possible. A good trial lawyer. *Very* good with a jury. I watched him quite a few times. I used to check with the courts to find out when his cases were coming up, and if I had time, I'd run over and watch. He was *real* good."

"Anything on his background? Where he was born? Where he grew up, went to school? How he got to the Peninsula?"

"Seems to me I heard he came from up north—Mendocino County, I think. I don't know much more. Except that somebody told me he went to West Point."

Another soldier. Maybe that was the key. Howard was about fifty when he died. He would have come out of the Military Academy in the early sixties, just the right time frame for Viet Nam.

"See what else you can dig up. I'm going to talk to the widow."

I called Joanna Gravesend. When I told her I wanted to come to the house for a chat, she seemed pretty cool to the idea. But I insisted. It was nine-thirty in the morning, and I told her I'd be at her place about ten.

The house that Howard had bought for Joanna was on a bluff facing the blue Pacific in an area known as Carmel Meadows. It's less than a mile south of the Carmel city limits, jutting out on a promontory that intrudes on the property of Carmel State Beach. Its desirability as a residential area is tempered somewhat by the fact that its streets are accessible only from Highway One on a stretch that becomes impossibly clogged at certain hours during the summer tourist season and the various holidays. It is possible, for instance, to be trapped for long periods of time when the northbound traffic into the Peninsula and points beyond is lined up as far as the eye can see, hung up on the traffic signals at Rio Road and Ocean Avenue.

I pulled up in front of the Gravesend house just as the 10 o'clock network news was coming from KCBS out of San Francisco. Joanna's silver Jaguar sedan was parked in the driveway, spotless and gleaming as usual. It always looked as if it had just been washed and polished.

She had apparently been watching for me. The door opened when I was halfway up the steps. She greeted me with a sweetly artificial smile and she was dressed in the high fashion, glistening as brightly as her automobile.

"You are prompt," she said, as she led me into the living room. "I hope this is something about the manuscript. You must have found Ed Summers."

"I'm sorry, Joanna. Summers is still AWOL, but we're checking his house. We can't find anybody who'll admit to being his friend." I omitted any reference to Summers' relationship with Arthur Wilson.

She looked puzzled... and a little irritated. "What is it then, Riordan? I hired you to find the Stevenson manuscript."

"We'll find it, we'll find it. The guy has to come back to the house. Unless he's dead." I immediately wished I hadn't said that. She jerked visibly, as if the idea of Summers' death was intolerable. "But I'm sure he's not," I added hastily.

"Then, what...."

"How much do you know about your late husband's background?"

"That's a hell of a question to ask. What does it have to do with anything?"

I was beginning to sweat. What was I going to say? How could I explain the Byzantine series of events that had occurred since Howard's death?

"I was just wondering if there was something in his past that could throw some light on the unusual circumstances of his death. Or maybe an old enemy somewhere. I still suspect foul play."

"Riordan, the sonofabitch got drunk, thought he was in a high diving contest, and busted his head because there wasn't any water in the pool, because there wasn't any pool. When are you going to understand?"

"Indulge me, Joanna. Just for a few minutes. When and where did you meet Howard?"

"At a party. In Pebble Beach. Fifteen years ago. My divorce had just become final. He was pointed out as single and eligible."

"I didn't know you had been married before."

"It's just as well. He was a world class jerk."

"What about Howard's life before he met you? Did he ever tell you anything?"

"Well . . . he was born in Fort Bragg. That's in Mendocino County. Not the military post in North Carolina."

"I know."

"He grew up there and in the town of Mendocino. That's a place about as arty as Carmel, only smaller. More fog, too, if you can believe it. He was pretty much of a barefoot boy, went to high school, got an appointment to West Point from some congressman his parents knew. Graduated in about the middle of his class in '61 or '62, I can't remember which. Went to Viet Nam, got shot up a couple of times, came back, got out, went to law school in San Francisco, came down here and started practicing with Alden. He was good in the court room, and in a couple of years, Alden made him a partner. How's that for a thumbnail sketch?"

"Nothing else?"

"He was a damn good trial attorney and a lousy husband. Everybody liked him, but nobody *cared* about him. He liked women, all shapes and sizes, . . . and golf. He could keep a party moving, but the guests were always glad to leave."

"The party where you met Howard in Pebble Beach—whose was it?"

"Oh, hell, Riordan, I've been to a thousand parties in Pebble Beach. I don't know. Wait. I remember. It was at Arthur Wilson's place."

16

"This is Summers. I hear you've been looking for me."

ARTHUR WILSON. The man keeps popping up in conversations. I thought about him as I drove back into Carmel. Either he is the most duplicitous character in the world, or I have lost my knack for character analysis. Maybe a little of both.

Reiko's elaborate computer outfit in the office is not one of Wilson's design. But I once picked up one of the hefty manuals that came with the machine and thumbed through it. I was convinced after a few pages that I could never understand the kind of mind that could design these infinitely complicated circuits. All old Tom Edison had to do was discover a filament that would endure the heat produced by the electric current he proposed to run through it. Voila! The light bulb! These computer whizzes have to create all this microscopic stuff that shuttles impulses around and makes sense out of them.

It's mind boggling. In my work I have a lot of contact with computer guys. A dozen Silicon Valley firms have used my services. I've had lunch with them, partied with them, and enjoyed their company. They tell jokes like real people. They make passes at each other's wives. They talk about golf (which I hate) and money (which I like). Only once in a while on these social occasions will several of them gather in a corner to converse in computerese, a language which, to me, might as well be Sanskrit. Outwardly, they seem to be completely normal. And most of them are Republicans.

At least, computer guys seem more normal to me than doctors. I had occasion once to attend a party at which most of the guests were doctors. Or *physicians* as they prefer to call themselves, to distinguish their profession from that of mere PhDs. I figured I'd learn something that evening, get some free medical advice if I listened to the conversations. So I drifted around with a glass of club soda in my hand and eavesdropped on conversations. Did I hear anything about medicine? Hell no, all the guys talked about was investments: condominiums, apartment complexes, office buildings, stocks and bonds. What would Hippocrates think? The Golden Age of Greece was never like this.

But computer people are like real human beings—at least, on the surface. Behind that facade of normalcy, though, must lurk some pretty devious minds, like those sneaky little invisible tracks on those tiny silicon chips. That would help to explain Arthur Wilson.

Driving up Rio Road into Carmel past the Mission, I became aware of a street across from the ball park that I must have driven past innumerable times, but had never noticed. It led straight up a hill whose height appeared from Rio Road to give an excellent view of the arrival of the Pope. I did a U-turn again at the Mission and drove back to climb Ladera Drive.

Later I learned that the street is within the Carmel city limits. But that was hard to believe from my first impression of large lots and expensive houses built to take advantage of the view. Building lots in Carmel are typically 40 by 100 feet. People build within these restrictions and try to make the most of them. If you want any more space, you leave the city limits, or you buy a couple of contiguous lots—if you can find them. As I reached the dead end at the top of Ladera Drive, I'd assessed the value of the houses at $700,000 and up—mostly up. I pulled up alongside a large open area near the top of the hill and got out. Walking to the edge where the grade began to get steep, I watched it all spread out below me: the Meadows, where I had visited Joanna, Point Lobos jutting out beyond, and, immediately below me, the Mission and the baseball field. If anybody wanted to get a shot at the Pope, this was the ideal place. A couple of sharpshooters, just to be sure, could accomplish such a task and disappear over the back of the hill into Mission Trails Park, or park a car on Trevis Way and, after a short run and a scramble up another slope, could be out on Highway One in seconds.

I shook my head sharply to get all this ridiculous fiction out of my mind. Why would anybody want to assassinate the Pope? Why, for God's sake, would Arthur Wilson or Lt. Col. Summers or, for that matter, Carlos Vesper want to assassinate the Pope? No way. Not a chance. Nada.

There was a movie called *The Day of the Jackal* a while back that had to do with an attempt to assassinate General Charles de Gaulle. It was pretty good, as I recall, full of suspense—even though you know de Gaulle isn't really going to get shot. The picture never really made clear why the killer had been hired to hit the General. But who cares, right? I once saw de Gaulle in a motorcade down Market Street in San Francisco, waving regally to the common people, most of whom either didn't care or didn't know who he was. There was more excitement when the Giants came to town from New York. Possibly the people who hired the "Jackal" were offended by sheer arrogance.

But who would want to kill the Pope? Oh, sure, a Bulgarian crackpot took a shot at him. And there are plenty of crackpots around.

I drove back over to Monterey, whistling tunes from Sondheim's *Pacific Overtures,* my all-time favorite stage musical, even though Reiko had to drag me to it kicking and screaming. The idea of a musical based on the opening of Japan after the two-and-a-half century isolation begun with the Tokugawa shogunate, was completely ridiculous. But I was enchanted, and I still am. Reiko had only been with me a couple of months when the show played San Francisco. And she was busy educating and reforming me.

She was straightening her desk and about to turn on the phone answering machine when I got back to the office.

"I was just going to lunch. Lenny will be here in two seconds."

Lenny was there in less than two seconds. He poked his blond head in the door as she spoke, and followed it in with his long, lean body. His puppy-dog adoration of Reiko shines in his terribly earnest eyes. Lenny and Reiko make quite a pair. He's pale, with freckles, and six-four or -five. Reiko, as you know, has to rock up on her toes to make five feet even. The two of them always attract a lot of attention on the street.

"Where are you going?"

Reiko looked up at Lenny. "Where, pal?"

"You name it."

"OK, the place over on Calle Principal. In the old fire house."

"It'll be crowded."

"Well, then, *you* pick a place." She was getting a little irritated.

"Anywhere's all right with me."

Reiko grabbed her purse. "Let's get the hell out of here." And I could see that no matter how fond she might be of Lenny, or he of her, it was a bad match. It was pretty much the same with all of her men friends. She didn't *mean* to intimidate them, but she did. Reiko was just too strong a personality for the available men in her age group. And she had an unalterable rule against dating married men. I can't see her as an elderly spinster in white hair and support hose. But it's going to take some kind of man to interest her enough to want to marry him.

After the young people had left, I sat down at my desk, leaned back and closed my eyes. I think I drifted off for a few minutes, because when the phone rang, I nearly tipped over backwards.

"Riordan," I said into the wrong end of my phone. Discovering my error, I repeated the name a second later.

The voice at the other end was hoarse and commanding. "This is Summers. I hear you've been looking for me."

17

"Maybe another time, sweetheart," I lisped . . .

Hᴇʀᴇ ᴡᴀs ᴀ guy who had dropped out of sight for a week, totally out of sight, whom Reiko and I had exhausted our collective resources trying to find. Here was the key man, the missing ingredient, the mystery voice that could tell many secrets. And *he* was calling *me*.

"Colonel Summers?" I asked, stupidly.

"You bet. So what's it all about?"

"Mrs. Gravesend—Joanna—was concerned about an item she left in your care. And when she couldn't find you. . . . "

"She figured I skipped with her poetry stuff, eh? Well, I got no use for the shit. What're you? Some kind of wimpy shamus?"

The word "shamus" is straight out of Hammett. I hadn't heard it for years, since my mentor, Al Jennings, who swore he had worked with the author for the Pinkertons in the old days, passed on to his reward, if any. I had suspected that Summers lived in a different world. "Wimpy" was something else. In an earlier time it would have sent me into a towering rage, and might have resulted in my tearing the phone off the wall. But I have learned to control myself.

"Colonel, I am a private investigator. I was engaged by Mrs. Graves-

80

end to do a job, nothing more. I will be glad to call on you so that you may turn the manuscript over to me. I will then deliver it to Mrs. Gravesend." I said all this through clenched teeth.

"In a pig's ass," said the Lieutenant Colonel, ret. "She wants her goddam poetry, I put it in *her* hands. She's a good lay, but a dumb broad. Hey, this Stevenson. Any relation to Adlai, that pinko egghead used to run for president?"

A gentleman and a scholar. Definitely not a poet. As an innocent, downy-cheeked private in Korea, I used to wonder about officers. Were they, indeed, a breed apart? Why did I have to do what they wanted me to do when I knew it was the wrong thing? I did it, surely, because I was a good soldier. A lot of good soldiers die. I was lucky.

Summers went on: "Meet me at three o'clock by the drug store at Ocean and Dolores. Have Joanna with you. I'll hand over the package. To *her,* not *you.*"

It was about a week before Labor Day. The weather was ideal: sunshine tempered by a gentle sea breeze, crystal air, not a hint of fog. It was the kind of Carmel day that stacks the cars bumper to bumper up Ocean Avenue to Highway One. Summers' designated meeting place is smack in the middle of the tourist traffic. There would be two hundred people going through that intersection every sixty seconds, all intent on finding Eastwood, crowding the locals (who only come in town in the summer to pick up their mail) off the sidewalks. I'm lucky enough to live north of Ocean, so I don't have to cross it to get to the post office.

I guess the crowd situation was Summers' idea of being crafty. Another devious bastard in a sort of Keystone Kop fashion. I was beginning to get flashes of Col. Flagg, the insane intelligence officer on M*A*S*H. That long ride that he gave Reiko when she was chasing him. God almighty, I thought, I bet he has a code name, something appropriate, like "The Eagle."

"Did you hear me, Riordan? Three o'clock. By the drug store."

"Aye, aye, sir," I said. I couldn't think of an appropriately subservient response from an ex-PFC to a Lt. Col., ret., so I made it nautical.

By the time I got Joanna on the phone it was ten after two.

"He wants to meet where?" she asked me in a disbelieving tone.

"You heard it. In a crowd. So we can't pull a knife on him, I guess.

I'm leaving now. You come to my place. It's at Sixth and Santa Rita, southwest corner."

"Is that a proposition, Riordan?" Her voice turned honey-smooth. I felt a flush rise from the back of my neck. "I'd guess we'd have about fifteen minutes to spare."

"Maybe another time, sweetheart," I lisped, doing my lousy Bogart. "We've got business to take care of."

"I'm leaving." She hung up abruptly.

I left the office, realized that I had parked some distance away and broke into a dog trot. My shirt was sweat-soaked when I reached the car, and I felt a pang at the thought of offending the highly polished Joanna with my odor. All the Estee Lauder cologne in my bathroom wouldn't do much good. The hell with it, I thought.

Nevertheless, when I got to the house, I hastily scrubbed my underarms with a washcloth, changed my shirt and underwear, and poured a small puddle of cologne into my hand, all in about two-and-a-half minutes.

The first thing Joanna said when she arrived was, "You smell like a second-rate Nevada whorehouse, Riordan."

This ruffled my feathers a bit. "I went to a lot of trouble to make myself sexually desirable and you complain about a little cologne."

"It's the cologne over the sweat, my friend. I am a fastidious person."

I shrugged. She didn't hire me to smell good.

We had time to walk down to the corner of Ocean and Dolores at a leisurely pace. The day was still bright and beautiful and the Pacific was blue. Vacationers and day-trippers crowded Ocean Avenue. Most of them were in shorts and T-shirts, many were eating something from one of the bakeries along the street, a surprising number were pushing or dragging small children who were not enjoying the day at all.

I counted on Joanna to recognize Summers when we met. I had never seen the man. We stood for a moment in front of the drug store, wondering what to do next. It was a minute or two before three.

The crowd was clogging the intersection. Tourists in Carmel saunter across the streets. At the intersection of Ocean and Dolores there is often a kind of gridlock: an unending stream of pedestrians in all four crosswalks, blocking vehicular traffic for two or three minutes at a time. Joanna and I stood there wondering. A young man on a skateboard lost his balance and pitched into me, knocking me against a magazine stand. I cried out in some anger, employing strong language. The kid glared, raised a middle finger at me, and rolled crazily on his way through the crowd.

At that moment a black Corvette slid up and stopped in the twenty-minute zone on Dolores, just at the corner. An arm and a head came out of the window on the passenger side. The hand on the arm clutched a brown envelope. The head was round and the hair—what there was of it—was clipped short. What could be seen of the face around the large dark glasses was deeply tanned and bore a thick, clipped black mustache. The sonofabitch *did* look like G. Gordon Liddy.

Summers grinned, showing a row of gleaming white teeth. He said nothing as Joanna took the envelope from him. He pulled his head and arm inside the car and muttered something to the driver, who took off through the intersection, scattering sightseers in all directions, causing one of them to let fly a half-eaten jelly doughnut that splattered on my clean shirt.

I scraped some of the goo off my chest, and licked my fingers. "So that was the mysterious Lt. Col. Summers, USA, ret. I thought at least I'd get a chance to ask him where the hell he's been."

Joanna was busy opening the package. She had pulled a sheaf of papers out of the envelope and was standing in the middle of the sidewalk examining them, oblivious to the tourist hordes milling around her.

Her eyes were wide when she looked at me. "This is nothing but a Xerox copy, Riordan. The whole manuscript run off on a copying machine. And this note." She handed me a sheet bearing a typed message.

I looked at the paper. The note was very military in form:

1300 hours, 26 August 1987

To: J. Gravesend
From: E. Summers, Lt. Col, USA, ret.
Subject: Poetry

The addressee is informed that if she wants her lousy poetry, she can make a substantial donation. $100,000 would be sufficient. A representative of the organization will be in touch.

18

"My God," I said,
"you sure are bowlegged."

W HAT DOES HE MEAN, 'the organization?' What organization? The Heart Fund? The Salvation Army? What kind of circus is
this, Riordan?" Joanna was standing in the middle of the sidewalk with
tears in her eyes. Her voice was too loud and passers-by looked at her
curiously. Here stood Joanna Gravesend, in a print Diane Freis dress,
navy pantyhose and high heels, at midafternoon on a late summer day
in Carmel, with her mascara beginning to run, almost shouting at me.

I took her by the elbow and led her up Ocean to the cocktail lounge
in the Doud Arcade. We sat in a dark, quiet corner in the back of the
room. Joanna had squeezed the manuscript copy into a wrinkled mess,
and was still clutching it tightly. Why I didn't look at it then I cannot
imagine. I might have . . . well, I didn't.

I tried to comfort her, but I could have used a little comforting
myself. "Joanna, there is a lot going on here that neither of us under-
stands completely. But I am beginning to put some facts together, and
I'm certain we'll have the answers very soon. Anyhow, now we've got
an extortion rap against Summers." I only lied a little. We did have a

criminal charge against Col. Summers, although I wasn't sure what kind of crime it was to hold poetry for ransom.

She calmed down after a bit, soothed by a vodka on the rocks with a squeeze of lime. I studied her face as she looked through the dark room to the bright light streaming in the open upper half of the Dutch door. This close-up look at Joanna confirmed an earlier observation that her face was not one I'd like to find on my pillow in the morning. As glamorous as she was, as easy as her reputation suggested, she just didn't turn me on, not even one little bit.

But halfway through her second vodka, she began to warm up. She moved closer and put her hand on mine.

"You know, Riordan, you're really a very attractive man. I know you and Sally have something going. But are you ... exclusive?"

"We've ... we've never really discussed the matter. Sally and I just sort of get along. We're not thinking of getting married or anything like that." It's Sally who rejects the idea of marriage. But I didn't say that. I was floundering. I looked at my watch. Actually, I can't tell what time it is without my glasses. But I faked it pretty well. "My God, Joanna, I'm supposed to meet a guy in my office at four-thirty. We'd better get going."

She gulped down the rest of her drink as I dragged her to her feet, and without another word, we left the bar and climbed the hill to my place where I gently put Joanna in her car, but not before she gave me an affectionate pat on the ass.

At another time, in another place, having a lady pat me on the *tuchus* would have started the motor running. But there was too much going on in my mind to respond with proper ardor to Joanna's touch. Besides, she was a little drunk, and I have found, in bitter experience, that booze may bring on the desire, but it impedes the performance. Sex, like the tango and gin rummy, is only good when practiced by two consenting, skillful adults.

Joanna left a trail of rubber as she zoomed up Sixth Avenue. I walked around to the front of the house and found Carlos Vesper sitting in a canvas chair on my deck, smoking a cigarette. He had apparently been there for some while. The deck was littered with squashed cigarette butts. He had a three-day beard and I could smell him from a distance of eight feet.

"What the hell are you doing here? I thought you were hiding out in San Francisco with a cellist. Either you are an incurable optimist or the flakiest con artist I have ever encountered."

"My conscience got the better of me, Riordan." I was not convinced. He dug his chin into his chest and rolled his eyes up at me. "I'm ready to make amends and apologize to those folks who had confidence in me. . . . "

"And give them their money back? Are you ready to do that, turkey?"

"Well, er, no. The money is gone. There's no way I could make that kind of restitution. I just thought. . . . "

"You're nuts, Carlos. Or you're lying. You took advantage of a lot of people who trusted you. They all lost a lot of money. At least one of them has bought a hit on you. And you want to *apologize?*"

He hung his head. "I guess you're right."

"You *know* I'm right! You came back here because you couldn't think of anyplace else to go. Your cello-playing lady friend probably tossed you out. You can't go back to your house in Monterey because Summers' thugs are watching it. But why me? Why on God's earth did you come here. And how did you find out where I live?"

"I . . . called your office. The woman who answered told me you'd be glad to see me."

Sweet, charming, ever-helpful Reiko. My partner, my brilliant partner. She thought I'd be glad to see Vesper. Now, why would I be glad to see Vesper? Reiko doesn't do *anything* without a good reason.

"Why would I be glad to see you?"

Vesper stood up, brushing cigarette ashes from his coat.

"Riordan, since Cynthia—the cellist—threw me out, I've been living on the street. You can do that in San Francisco, but it isn't very comfortable. Do you suppose I could use your bathroom—take a shower, borrow some clothes?"

I shrugged. Nothing much I could do. "OK. I'm curious, though. Why did your cellist throw you out?"

He stubbed out the cigarette he had been smoking on the edge of a planter box.

"You know she had these great knees. When she was playing on the stage at Davies I couldn't take my eyes off her knees. But the second night I was with her, she got out of bed to go to the john. I couldn't help myself. 'My God,', I said, 'you sure are bowlegged!' This was not really the proper thing to do. But it was such a tremendous shock. Although I guess it's an advantage to a cellist."

He had such an innocent smile. No wonder he had been able to wheedle money out of a lot of reasonably intelligent people. I couldn't help being amused, but I didn't want to show him that.

"I'm going to ask you again, Carlos. Why did Reiko think I'd be glad to see you?

I was holding the door of the house open for him. Just inside the entry, he turned. The smile was gone.

"When I was putting together the group to make a move on Omicron, I did a lot of digging on Arthur Wilson. And you know something? He had a lot of very strange connections. Arthur the Genius is not the patriotic saint he appears to be. The woman in your office thought you'd like to know that."

19

"I have lived a lot for a young man, Riordan," he said.

WELL, IT wasn't something I didn't already know. Arthur Wilson was into some kind of activity with the hard-guy Lt. Col. Ed Summers. The two of them went way back and had been jointly involved with an organization that sounded very right-wing militant, indeed. But Wilson was such a pleasant, quiet-spoken guy—so different from the Colonel, who radiated menace in the few moments I had come in contact with him. I didn't know what Vesper could tell me that I didn't already know, or suspect. I showed the man the way to the bathroom, warned him about the makeshift shower that sometimes sends a torrent out the window if not aimed properly, dug out a pair of old jeans and some raggedy underwear that I had set aside to polish the car with—if I ever got around to polishing the car—and sat down in my kitchen to wait and meditate.

I am pretty deep into some serious activity, I reflected. A man could get hurt. All during my career as an investigator, a profession I fell into rather than chose, I have steered clear of violence. I watch these guys on TV on the private eye shows always getting into fist-fights and gun battles, and I wonder how they pay their rent. You can't make any money chasing bad guys with guns. You know you aren't going to get paid by the beautiful chick with the big bazooms. Joanna Gravesend was really the only woman who ever came into my office even slightly on the make. I might have been a taker, but her eyes are too close together and she's got a skinny behind.

Over in a corner of my office in an elephant's foot umbrella holder left me by my mentor Al Jennings, is a blackthorn walking stick that my late wife bought for me from an Irish import shop. Whenever I feel that I might get into a tight situation, I take along the stick. Not that it could do me much good against, say, an Uzi. But it gives me a misguided sense of security. The fact is, I could carry a gun if I wanted to. Tony Balestreri, my friend in the Sheriff's office, has begged me to apply for a permit. But I do not like guns. Guns scare me. People like Col. Summers scare me. And I don't feel particularly bad about that. The weeks I spent on the front line in Korea, exposed daily to gunfire and shellfire taught me that guns are good for one thing: putting holes in people. Guys with holes in them were all around me, some of them living and bleeding, some of them mercifully dead. I swore that as soon as I could get rid of the rifle I was obliged to carry, I would never touch another gun.

I sat waiting for Vesper to come downstairs and wondered if I weren't a little foolish even to put up with the guy in my own home. After all I had heard about him from Sally and others, I had to figure that this was one of the luckiest guys around. Sal had gone on and on about his charm. He had fleeced a lot of nice people. But my own impression of him was that he was a sort of taller Dudley Moore type, with a facile, surface attractiveness, no sense of morality, and a gift for finding the right place at the right time.

He came down the stairs, toweling his hair. My jeans were a little loose on him, but he had appropriated a cord that had been attached to a fancy shell-shaped bar of shower soap that Sally had given me and I had never used, and had made a makeshift belt.

"What did you do with the soap?"

"What soap?"

"The soap that was hanging on that cord."

"Oh. Well, I was kind of desperate, you know. And you hadn't used the soap."

"It *had* to hang there, goddammit. My girl gave it to me and she liked to see it hanging there."

"And she could see well enough you'd never used it, couldn't she?"

He had me there. He walked over to my couch and sat down, stretching his legs out with his bare heels on the floor.

"I have lived a lot for a young man, Riordan," he said. "I have been to Europe a number of times. I have a Swiss numbered bank account. Of course, it's hung up now because thirty or forty people are suing me. But how many other people do you know who have Swiss numbered bank accounts? No matter. How many other people have ever had a Lamborghini Countach repossessed? How many other people have defaulted on a five-hundred thousand dollar mortgage? Yes, I have enjoyed a remarkable degree of success."

He actually seemed pleased with himself. It didn't matter that he was in deep trouble or that his life was threatened. Carlos Vesper is a creature of his times. It doesn't matter how you get it just so you get it. And if you lose it, you can just get it again. I thought, if this guy ever gets out from under his current troubles, he'll have that Lamborghini back again.

"But you want to know about Arthur Wilson. What I found out about Arthur Wilson, right?"

"Let's have it, Carlos."

"You got a cigarette?"

"Don't use 'em."

"Pity. Oh, well, you know what the surgeon general says. Riordan, Arthur Wilson—aside from being a genius in the field of electronics—is a *bigot* of the worst order." He nodded at me sagely. He was about to impart some really shocking information. He frowned and pursed his lips.

"That's not really a criminal offense, Carlos."

"There's more. Wilson over the years has evolved from being an ultra-conservative manufacturer into being a full-fledged Neo-Nazi."

"Bullshit."

"It's true. That is why he hooked up with Colonel Ed Summers. Admittedly, they were old associates in the Reserve, but now they are full partners."

"Partners in what?"

"In a conspiracy to rid the world of it's most evil influence."

"What? The Jews? The Communists? The Democratic Party?"

Vesper sat up and leaned forward. His eyes opened wide and his voice was a hoarse whisper.

"The Vatican," he said.

20

"There was another name mentioned. Highbridge."

YOU KNOW, I was expecting that. All the cloak-and-dagger stuff that had been going on was much too obvious to be just an exercise. The liaison between Arthur Wilson and Lt. Col. Edward Summers, USA, ret. was too much to ignore. The imminent visit of the Pope was an event of global importance. And these guys, with their recruits drawn from all parts of the country, were going to try to kill the Pope. Or they *thought* they were going to try to kill the Pope. What a marvelous opportunity for a small-time bunch of toy soldiers to make a big statement. Golly, gang, we can all get together and kill that old Polack and make the world safe for . . . what?

It seems that nothing goes on around this world that doesn't draw a protest. Not often a *lethal* protest, but a display of righteous indignation. I have a notion that at any given demonstration you might be able to draw a placard-carrying protester aside and ask him what it was all about and get a shrug for your pains.

If Carlos Vesper was telling me the truth about Wilson, I had no doubt that Wilson really believed that the Vatican was a source of evil in the world. He could probably tell me in his smooth, articulate way, that there were good and valid reasons to eliminate the Pope. And it wouldn't do any good for me (or anybody else) to try to argue against him. I had always believed that the men of conviction behind terrorist acts were absolutely certain in their beliefs—certain, unemotional, logical, ruthless. You could sit down and have a cup of coffee with one of them, and enjoy the conversation. You'd laugh, and tell a few jokes, and talk about what happened to the Giants, and never know that the guy was planning to blow up a department store the next morning.

So, assuming Vesper's information was accurate, it would do no good to go to Wilson and try to talk him out of it. When Vesper laid this burden on me, the papal visit was under two weeks away. Plans had already been made. Summers was hiding out somewhere, along with his broken-nosed recruits. Military professionals rehearse their blood-letting exercises down to the last detail. And there were plenty of woodsy canyons around Big Sur where Summers and his would-be mercenaries could do their dry runs.

"Would you like a drink, Carlos?"

"You got Chivas Regal?"

"I've got half a bottle of no-name bourbon that's been around here for two years, take it or leave it."

"OK. With 7-Up."

Although I have not had a drink for ten years, I still wince when somebody drinks booze mixed with soda-pop.

"No 7-Up. Water or over ice or straight. No mixers at all."

Vesper sighed. "Water," he said.

From the cabinet over the sink, I took down the dusty bottle of supermarket bourbon, poured him an inch and a half in a glass, and splashed water in it from the tap.

He sipped some of the mixture with a wry look on his face, and coughed gently to let me know it was something he wasn't used to. He shuddered, albeit discreetly.

"Could we have a fire, Riordan? I'm getting a little chilled."

I went to the closet and got him an old sweatshirt I use for slopping around the house. There was dry wood in a basket on the hearth, so I threw a couple of logs in the fireplace along with some old newspapers. In a couple of minutes there was a cheerful fire. The only problem with fireplaces in these old houses is that often there are no dampers, and a stiff wind from the outside can blow the smoke—and sometimes the fire—back into the living room.

I sat down on the couch beside Carlos. "What else do you know about Wilson? Aside from his religious bigotry."

"I told you before—when you blocked my driveway—that I'd heard the guy was running out of dough. I made some inquiries. You know, when I was putting together a group to make a move on Omicron. Can't tell you the sources but the word was that Wilson was bankrolling a sort of independent army. He was originally going to rid Central America of communists, but he figured it would take more cash than he could raise. Then he started reading about the way the Catholic church was behaving in Nicaragua, he figured he could specialize. And when the word began to circulate that the Pope was going to visit Monterey County, he saw his golden opportunity. He wouldn't have to risk a lot of capital to knock off a few lousy bishops. He'd get right to the top. The head man."

Something was rattling around in the back of my mind. "I had a visit from a couple of three-piece suits named Schneider and Stramm. They put me on to you as a key man in the takeover maneuver. Are they involved in this weirdness?"

"Oh, no, they're just corporate errand-boys, with nothing on their minds except getting to the top through hard work and integrity. Couple of real horse's asses."

"There was another name mentioned. Highbridge. A guy who was in on the takeover with you. Local guy."

Vesper showed genuine surprise. "How did those two turkeys get that name? They must be a lot smarter than I thought."

"Well? What about Highbridge?"

Vesper ran his fingers through his still-damp hair. "Alonzo Highbridge. A director of the Farmers' and Ranchers' Bank over in Hollister. Agribusinessman, lettuce speculator. In his sixties, but not old, know what I mean. I got to him through Joanna Gravesend. I think she was sleeping with him every now and than. He lives in Salinas. No big show. Lives in a house that needs paint. But he's got enough in the bank to *buy* Carmel. And that's just in his checking account."

"If Highbridge has all these assets, why in hell did you have to go to San Jose to recruit partners for the Omicron takeover?"

"He's an astute man, Riordan. A little dab of this, a little dab of that. He has only two interests: money and women, in that precise order. Managing money is his fun, and it helps him to manage the women. Drives an old Mercury with dents in the rear fenders. That Ford wagon I was loading up when you came to my house, that was his. What a guy."

Vesper had a look of sheer admiration on his face. The acquisition of money, I'm sure, was the trait he most admired in Highbridge. What a lot of Lamborghinis that kind of money could buy—outright.

"You say you got in touch with Highbridge through Joanna. How did Joanna get involved with him?"

"Her husband did some legal work for him. I'm not sure about the details, but it involved a criminal charge, I think. Joanna's husband defended Highbridge's son—and got him off. Then they got kind of chummy, Highbridge would visit them at the Point house, and pretty soon Joanna was spending nights with him."

"Did Highbridge know Arthur Wilson?"

"Yeah, that's the funny thing about it. He and Arthur had gone to college together. At Stanford. Maybe they were roommates, I don't remember. But much later, in business, Wilson did something that Highbridge did not like at all. Lost him a lot of money, but that wasn't what bothered him. The fact that Wilson betrayed him made him furious. He never told me what that was, but he would have been happy to have Wilson's hide nailed to the barn door. I think the only person who knew the real reason for all this hate was Howard Gravesend."

21

"One does not get to be a millionaire by being nice, Reiko-san."

By THIS TIME, the shades of night were falling fast, and I was getting hungry. I didn't feel like buying Vesper dinner, so I opened a couple of cans of different kinds of soup, poured them together into a saucepan and heated the mess up. This, together with a box of stale water biscuits I had bought to eat with a wedge of brie Sally had given me, was our meal. We topped it off with what was left of a quart of chocolate-peanut-butter ice cream I found pushed to the back of the freezing compartment of my refrigerator.

"Want some coffee? I got some decaffeinated beans. Have to grind 'em."

Vesper, who had regained his position on the couch after dinner, didn't answer. He had slumped against the cushions of the couch and almost immediately fallen asleep.

I went upstairs and pulled a blanket out of my closet and covered the sleeping Vesper. He'd had a rough time of it since his madonna of the string section threw him out. But that's what you have to expect from musicians. Super-sensitivity.

Sleep does not come to me at seven o'clock in the evening. Even if I am very tired, I cannot go to sleep at such an hour. My head is geared for sleep to come after the eleven o'clock news, and it just won't happen any earlier. Besides, my mind was racing with the addition to the cast of characters of an intriguing newcomer.

I called Reiko. After five rings, just as I was about to abandon the call, she came on the line:

"Hello!" She sounded angry.

"Reiko-san, it is indeed good to hear your voice. I was afraid I had missed you."

"Riordan, goddammit, I was washing my hair. Water is running down the back of my neck. I hope you have something important to say. Hang on a minute."

The phone clattered on a desk top or a table and there was silence for a minute or so. When next she spoke, she was a little more composed.

"So? You monopolize my services during the day, and you invade my privacy at night. What have I done to deserve this sort of treatment."

"You are my partner, shrewish one. You must learn to expect phone calls at inconvenient moments. I might even call you when you are *in flagrante delicto* with some undeserving youth."

"I don't do *delicto* and I don't do windows. What's on your mind?"

"Know anything about Alonzo Highbridge? I just got some interesting information from Carlos Vesper...."

"Can't you remember *anything*? I told you he was one of the guys Joanna Gravesend was sleeping with. The sixty-four-year-old lettuce magnate. Probably on goat serum or massive doses of vitamin E, who knows? What else do you need to know?"

"You didn't mention his name, as I recall. Aside from his bedroom proclivities, do you have anything else?"

There was a momentary pause at the other end of the line. "I really didn't get much beyond the fact that he was laying Joanna on a regular basis. Let me check my notes." I heard a drawer slide open and the rustle of papers. "I've got a whole bunch of stuff here on Summers. And there was that insurance salesman in Marina. That might have been a one-night stand. And the guard from Soledad. What a stud! Oh, here's something. In checking out Highbridge, I found out that Howard, Joanna's husband, had defended his son on an embezzlement charge and got him off. I thought that was peculiar at the time. You know I didn't like Howard very much, but for Highbridge to show his gratitude by humping Joanna—well, now, that's not very nice."

"One does not get to be a multi-millionaire by being nice, Reiko-san. Remember the words of the immortal Leo Durocher, 'Nice guys don't win ball games', or something to that effect."

"Who's Leo Durocher?"

"An old shortstop. Forget it, young person. Did you uncover any possible connection between Highbridge and Summers?"

"Negative. Highbridge is a respectable Salinas businessman. Lives modestly. His only apparent indulgence is golf. If you eliminate women. He belongs to the Cypress Point club. Plays regularly—maybe two, three times a week—with a bunch of moneybags. He'll drive over here early in the morning, play his rounds, and drive back to Salinas. He never stays on the Peninsula very long."

"How about Arthur Wilson? Get anything on Highbridge's relationship with Wilson? I understand they were sworn enemies."

"Let me look. Yeah, Riordan, they were partners once. When Wilson was just beginning to get big. This isn't clear, but what I got was that somehow or other, just as Wilson was about to get into the really *big* money, he eased Highbridge out in some kind of corporate maneuver. Highbridge beat up on him in the boardroom, but nothing could be done about it."

"Meet me in the office in the morning, Reiko-san. There's an awful lot to do."

"OK. You buy some croissants."

I hung up. There really wasn't much I could do, although I felt that there were things going on out there that I really ought to stop. Vesper was snoring on my couch. I dialed the Carmel Police business number.

"Lieutenant Miller?"

"I'm sorry, he's out cruising. He's on supervision tonight."

I thought of big-shouldered John Miller out "cruising" in the gay sense of the word, and I giggled. "Would you get a message to him? This is *not* an emergency. Tell him that Pat Riordan needs to talk to him at his earliest convenience."

"I'll give him a call, Mr. Riordan."

In about fifteen minutes, less time than it took me to fix that mess of mixed pottage for dinner, Miller was knocking on my door.

"What's up, Pat. Got your call. You got a barking dog or a cat up a tree? Your neighbors playing acid rock on the stereo too loud. Some kind of real Carmel complaint?"

I motioned the Lieutenant into the kitchen, gesturing at the sleeping Vesper as we passed the couch.

"I don't think he's a fugitive from justice, but there are some guys out there looking to break his legs."

"Isn't that Vesper, the character everybody's suing? My in-laws dropped twenty thousand dollars with the sonofabitch."

"Yes, John, he is an unsavory character—but he's not what I called you about. Remember when we talked about the Pope's visit. It's less than two weeks away now, you know."

Miller's shoulders sagged. "I don't have to be reminded. I get new information every day, and it all has to be checked out. Now there's a crazy FBI guy over in Monterey who keeps ragging us on the telephone. Is that all you wanted? To let me know what I already know?"

I took a deep breath. "I don't want to burden you with more hassle than is necessary. But in my bumbling way, I have uncovered what I think must be a plot to kill the Pope."

"Get in line. Just today I have been made aware of four calls indicating that same possibility. Every nut in Monterey County is planning to shoot the Pope. Or flood the ball park when he lands with poison gas. Or kidnap him and fly him to Venus."

I shook my head and tried to look as grave as possible. "This is legit, John. I have reason to believe that a group of men, including Lt. Col. Edward Summers, of whom we spoke, and a prominent Peninsula businessman, have concocted a plot to assassinate the Pope. I'm not sure why. I'm not even sure *they* know why. And I'm not easily disturbed by the bizarre."

"Are you serious?" Miller was incredulous. His mouth hung open, and he put his hand on his gun. That gave me a jerk.

"I have never been more serious, and you don't have to draw on me. I'm unarmed."

"I'm sorry, Pat. It's a policeman's reaction to shock. The gun is sort of a comfort, I guess. How do these guys propose to pull it off?"

"That I don't know. But I have a suggestion. There's a vacant lot at the top of Ladera Drive, and.... "

"We've got that covered, Pat. That and Mission Trails Park, the perimeter of the ball field, the Mission School playground, all of Rio Road. A couple of choppers from Fort Ord will be in the vicinity. It's all tight. No way anybody's going to get off a shot. Not a chance."

He didn't look all that sure about it, though. I noticed small beads of perspiration on his popping out at his temples and on his upper lip. Sort of like Richard Nixon at a press conference.

"I hope you're right. But Summers is a professional. He is an experienced killer. I can only assume that the guys he's got working for him are disciplined professionals, also. If I'm right, an attempt will be made. You've covered just about everything. Fine. But how many assassinations can you think of when everything's been covered, but it happened anyway. Both Kennedys, Sadat, Aquino, Martin Luther King. I'm sorry, John, to burden you with this, but we've got less than two weeks to cover every angle."

22

"The world is full of crazies. And often they look like you and me, kid."

WHEN JOHN MILLER left, I went to bed without disturbing Vesper, who was blissfully sawing logs on my couch. I have a little black-and-white TV in my bedroom upstairs, and I watched a two hour stretch of a one hour story, based on a fifteen minute plot that would have made a pretty good 30-second spot. TV is very like Parkinson's Law: the material expands in order to fill the time alloted.

In the morning, Vesper was still asleep on my couch. He had hardly changed position. The few days he spent on the street in San Francisco exhausted him, but the experience apparently had not taught him anything. I had the impression that he would do it all over again without a qualm. What next, after worthless securities? Submerged vacation property in Florida? Non-existent oil reserves in Texas? Carlos is one of those enviable characters who can always land on his feet, even if it's in a vat of fertilizer.

When I got to the office, Reiko was there, shuffling through an enormous pile of papers on her desk. She looked up as I came through the door.

"My notes. I write 'em out on yellow legal pads and then transcribe 'em on my typewriter at home. I'd rather use a computer, but the guy I work for doesn't pay me enough to buy a laptop job for homework."

"Your grandfather left you a goodly chunk, Reiko-san. Why don't you loosen up a little with it instead of laying a guilt trip on me?"

"My grandfather's will stipulated that the money be in certificates of deposit and government securities. I remember his telling me that it would grow like the flowers of the garden, if properly nurtured. I'm not going to touch any of it until I get married. Or maybe when my first child is born. Or. . . ."

"Commendable advice. Do as grandpa said. Anyhow, now you're my partner, you're entitled to half the profits of this company."

"What profits? We've been lucky to break even and pay our bills. You pull a salary and I pull a mere pittance and the rest of the revenue goes for rent and the light bill. With all those filthy rich people you do business with, I'd suppose you could raise your—*our*—rates a few bucks."

"Why are we bickering, Reiko-san? We have work to do, miles to go before we sleep. What do you know that's new?"

She consulted a note. "About that missing manuscript. The poems by Robert Louis Stevenson. Probably a phony in the first place. He was here only a few months, didn't know many local people, spent most of his time with Mrs. Osbourne, the married lady he chased here. I got his *Collected Poems* out of the library, and, believe it, aside from the children's verses he wrote, he wasn't that much of a poet. I think Joanna's grandfather or great-grandfather, whichever, hoked up the whole thing. So who cares if Colonel Summers has the 'original'?"

She paused and frowned. From her desk drawer she drew a large pair of black rimmed spectacles which she placed with a flourish on her small nose. She gave me a steely glance that clearly said, "Don't say a word, sucker, or I'll punch you in the mouth!"

"With respect to the traditions of Monterey Bay, I will officially designate the Stevenson manuscript as a red sardine. But Joanna really believes in it and I don't want to be the one to tell her it's a fake."

"So what else, partner?"

"With a little bit of help from my family, I checked out the true financial condition of Omicron Megabyte Systems. Although Arthur Wilson may have been hard hit personally in recent months, Omicron is solid as a rock. And it is about to spring some sort of revolutionary device on the world. Security is in the hands of the two who came here, Schneider and Stramm. Schneider is a kind of fussbudget, but Stramm, despite his sloppy look and disengaged attitude, is one tough cookie. Believe it or not, he is an ex-CIA man. How's that for a dash of adventure?"

"Anything else?" I was awestruck, but I didn't want her to know it.

"Nothing new on Summers and the gang. Nothing you don't already know about Arthur Wilson. Highbridge we talked about last night. What have you got?"

I told her about the visit of Carlos Vesper and his revelations about Wilson. She whistled softly.

"Is that what this Summers thing is all about. All those guys over at the picnic grounds on Arroyo Seco Road are part of a terrorist gang preparing to off the Pope? You got to be kidding, Riordan."

"I honestly don't know. The world is full of crazies. And often they look like you and me, kid. I find it bordering on the sacrilegious to suspect such a thing of Arthur Wilson. But these are the eighties. Anything can happen, and probably will."

I was sitting on her desk, for a change. She got up from her chair and sat beside me, putting her warm hand on mine. "I've never seen you so serious," she said. "This thing has really got to you, hasn't it?"

I put my arm around her shoulders. "Reiko-san, I was hired originally to do a routine divorce job. That's my speed. I know what to do. Then my client gets himself killed. In a few weeks I'm involved in a series of events that would make Mike Flaherty drool. A week from next Thursday, what happens in Carmel will be front page news all over the world. And I have information, true or false, that scares the hell out of me. And I'm not sure I know what to do about it."

"How about consulting an expert?"

"Expert? Who the hell do I know that's an expert?"

She stood before me, taking both of my hands in hers and grinned owlishly behind those enormous glasses. "One of our best friends, Riordan. A guy who did two tours in Viet Nam in the Airborne Combat Engineers. Who got shot up and blown up and lived to tell the tale. Greg Farrell."

23

"You going to start your own war, Pat?"

I DON'T QUITE KNOW what to tell you about Greg Farrell. He is a singular soul, an artist, a soldier, a lover, a connoisseur of tropical fish and fine poultry. Our friendship goes back about fifteen years, ever since Helen, my late wife, decided to take up oil painting. Greg was teaching a class on Tuesday mornings at the Sunset Center, Carmel's hub of activities, an old school complex somewhat in need of repairs. We used to spend a lot of time in Carmel in those days. Helen was a buyer for a high fashion ladies' garment chain and could pretty much control her working time. I was muddling along in my investigative career, such as it was, and didn't need to do anything to take the day off but close and lock my office door.

Helen's income was greater and somewhat more regular than mine. But that never disturbed her. I couldn't understand why she married me, and I asked her one day. "It's your naivete, Riordan. I just adore your naivete. You pretend to be Humphrey Bogart, and you're more like Charlie Brown." She laughed and kissed me lightly on the forehead. I still get a terrible hollowness in my gut when I think about her. And she's been gone . . . my God, over ten years.

We'd pack up and drive to Carmel on Monday nights in the summer time, get a room at the Pine Inn and have a good dinner at

Casanova or the Swiss Tavern. Next morning I'd deliver my wife to Sunset Center, then wander off to loaf until noon in the village. Then we'd drive back in the afternoon. It was great for breaking up the week. We both had to be on the job Saturdays and sometimes Sundays, so taking Tuesday off was no big deal.

I began sitting in on Greg's lectures. He was very good at what he did. Each week he'd select a painter he admired and study up. Then he'd spend the first hour or so of his class talking about the painter's background and technique. We asked him to have lunch with us a couple of times. We bought a few of his paintings. We became good friends.

He was a hard guy to get to know well. It was a long time before he took us into his confidence. Years, as a matter of fact. When we did learn about him, it was a surprise to both of us.

Greg doesn't teach any more. Teaching, I learned long after I first met him, was not his cup of tea. He felt frustrated with students, most of whom were women in middle age and beyond. He didn't demonstrate—he refuses to let anybody watch him paint—and he wouldn't tell a student stroke for stroke what to do. He prefers the seclusion of his own studio, in a canyon halfway to Big Sur, where he can work undisturbed and paint what he wants to paint.

He has lived in his canyon retreat without benefit of the accepted comforts for years. He uses bottled gas for cooking, water from the mountains that rise sharply behind his house, and raises domestic fowl for food. For the first seven or eight years, he spent his evenings listening to classical music, or reading the books he collected from used book stores all over the Peninsula. Now, however, thanks to a windfall from an avid collector, he owns a TV and *two* VCRs. He can't get any television reception from the great outside world, but he makes a trip into town once or twice a week to rent video cassettes, makes copies of them and adds them to his library.

Since I have come to know him well, I have learned that he is not only an old soldier, an accomplished artist, and a devil with the ladies. He is a true philosopher, a lover of knowledge. When something takes his interest, he makes himself an expert on the subject. And his interests are eclectic.

What I needed to help me find my way through the thicket of plots

I found myself in was Greg's military expertise. If *he* were in charge of a plot to assassinate the Pope, what would he do?

I punched out his number on the phone. After eight rings, he came on breathlessly.

"Farrell. Go ahead."

"Greg, this is Riordan. How are you?"

"Pat, you don't really want to know how I am. You never call me to find out how I am. Cut to the chase. What do you want?"

This was Farrell the movie fan using a familiar TV expression. "Cut to the chase." I found out later that an admiring female was taping some of the more popular TV shows for him and hoping that she would be asked to deliver them in person.

"Why don't you say something more businesslike, like 'get to the bottom line?' You sound like a shoestring producer."

"I am in the middle of a painting. Do I call you when you're deeply involved in whatever it is you do?"

"I need your help. You know military tactics. I have a problem for you to solve."

"Have I missed something? Have we declared war on the Bahamas? What kind of problem?"

"I'll have to see you, Greg. Can't really do it on the phone."

There was a pause and a barely detectible sigh. "Come on down. In a couple of hours. I'll need that much time to finish what I'm doing. If I stop now I'll lose it."

I thanked him effusively and hung up. It was eight-thirty by my office clock—which meant it was nearer eight-forty-five. The drive to Greg's takes about a half hour. That meant I had until quarter to eleven to catch up on some old stuff in the office that I had been neglecting in recent days. *And* that it would be noonish when I got to Greg's. I made a mental note to stop at Garzone's delicatessen and pick up a couple of sandwiches. Greg never had anything in his refrigerator, and I didn't want to have to take him to the Rocky Point Restaurant for lunch. It's a great place, but you pay for the view.

I am never altogether comfortable driving down Highway One. It is narrow, it is winding, and people drive too damned fast. It seems like just about every other day that an ambulance runs out of Carmel down the highway, lights ablaze, sirens screaming. Tony Balestreri told me once that the people who cause most of the accidents are locals. They get so frustrated with the sightseers, gawking and pointing at the fabulous scenery, that they just open it up and blast off. This usually produces a multi-car pile-up, often with serious results.

When I finished my paper work in the office, I went to my car, checked the fuel gauge, kicked the tires, and rolled off in the direction of Big Sur. It was almost the middle of September, I reasoned, and there wouldn't be that much traffic on the road. I was right. Past Monastery Beach everything cleared up and I made excellent time to Greg's place.

I found him in his studio, standing motionless before an unfinished painting, his right hand clutching a brush as if it were a stiletto.

"You going to slash your painting, Vincent? Or cut off your ear? You got a few bucks worth of oil and canvas there, baby. Paint it over again."

Greg turned and looked at me blankly. He was in that creative semi-trance that overtook him when he had the big idea. I'd seen him in that state before.

"I thought I told you to wait a couple of hours," he said in a hoarse whisper.

"It has been more than a couple of hours, Greg. I drank three cups of coffee, wrote a couple of reports, and took a leisurely drive down the coast. What more could you ask?"

With a sad little smile, he put down his brush and picked up a turpentine-soaked rag. He wiped his hands very carefully, rubbing them with the rag perhaps longer than was absolutely necessary. "It was there for a little while, Pat. I don't know what happened. You made me answer the phone, goddammit, and it went. Oh, shit, it wasn't your fault. Maybe I'm losing it."

"Maybe you need a break, maestro. Maybe you need a wife. Or an uninhibited roll in the hay with a blonde cheerleader. You're burning up some of the best years of your life in this solitary existence."

"Wasn't solitary last night, Pat. I met this little schoolteacher at a bar in Carmel, and you know I couldn't believe it. I didn't know schoolteachers did things like that. Why, she—"

"Spare me the details. Obviously your love life is rolling along satisfactorily. Now, I need your hard- bought knowledge of jungle warfare."

"You're too old to volunteer. Why in hell do you want to know about military science and tactics?"

"Korea is a long time ago. And all I can remember is being shot at and freezing my ass. Besides, I was a PFC rifleman. I just did what they told me to do. You were an officer. You were the one to make the decisions. You were in on the planning."

"You going to start your own war, Pat? What kind of planning do you need?"

I told him about my nagging concern that a bunch of hired soldiers were going to try to hit the Pope. He listened intently as I described Lt. Col. Edward Summers, USA, ret., and his merry band. He displayed no emotion as I related the connection with the well-respected Arthur Wilson.

"So who's Wilson?" was all I got out of him. I had to explain *that*.

"I've been all over the potential scene of the crime, Greg. The man is landing in a helicopter on the baseball field next to the Mission property. On the one hand it looks like a very vulnerable spot. On the other, there'll be hundreds of cops around and a crowd nobody can even guess at right now."

Greg looked thoughtful. "This isn't the jungle, you understand. God knows we can't strip the trees with Agent Orange. The Carmel Forestry Department would have a fit. Let's go up and take a look around."

He deliberately cleaned the brushes he had been using, took one long last look at his unfinished painting, and started out of the studio. For the first time I took a hard look at what he had been working on. A well-upholstered naked lady was on her hands and knees crawling away from me, with her rosy buttocks prominently and temptingly displayed center foreground. I resisted a strong urge to pat the round bottom. Besides, the paint was still wet.

When I opened the passenger door of the Mercedes, Greg gave me a disdainful look. "We take the truck. Who ever heard of a military mission in a 450SL?"

Obediently, I got into his black pickup and we took off up the coast at a furious pace. The vehicle has no seat belts, and I got a firm grip on whatever I could find and after a couple of miles, was able to open my eyes.

When we got near the Mission, he slowed down. We rolled into the parking lot, already filled with tourist cars. We parked alongside the baseball field while Greg studied the territory. "Wait here," he said, like a real combat officer, and strode off across the field. He was silent and thoughtful when he returned. He drove up Ladera Drive, gunning the truck intentionally, I think, so the damaged muffler would make as much noise as possible. He said nothing. We walked together to the edge of the vacant lot overlooking the Mission and peered down at the Pope's destination.

Silently, we got back in the car and drove down to Rio Road. "I'm hungry," he said. I thought of the sandwiches I had taken down to his house, still in a package on the seat of the Mercedes.

"I'll buy you a hamburger at Chutney's," I said, reluctantly. He seemed pleased.

We drove over to the restaurant in the Crossroads Shopping Center. Greg seemed to be wrestling with his thoughts on the military operation I had asked him about. Once in a while he would mutter something unintelligible. He obviously wasn't talking to me—or anybody else. He was in the grip of a great problem, and his frown suggested that the solution was not an easy one.

All through our lunch he sat silent. The ample hamburger and all the trimmings vanished in a matter of minutes. He washed it all down with several huge glasses of iced tea. I nursed a decent green salad. All the dishes at Chutney's are prepared with a lot of imagination. I go there often. But that day I didn't think I was hungry.

On our way out, each of us grabbed a toothpick, and Greg used his with great skill and concentration all the way to the truck.

Finally, he spoke. "No way, Patrick. If the authorities have this place covered as well as you say they have, there is no way anybody can get a shot at the man. Unless, of course, they are religious fanatics and realize they're going to get killed on the spot if they try. That's heaven insurance. To die in the service of the faith is a supersonic flight to the promised land."

"These guys are not fanatics. I'm not sure what they *are*, but I don't think they're even church members."

"The only way they could even come close is with mortar fire," he mused, with a faraway look in his eye. "A spot on the reverse side of one of these hills wouldn't be hard to find. But it would take some practice. And where are they going to practice?"

"So, your conclusion is that this possible conspiracy to assassinate the Pope cannot be pulled off. Even by a combat-wise pair like Arthur Wilson and Ed Summers?"

Greg stretched. "Anybody who would try an operation like that has got to be stupid. Experience, hell. They've got to be dumber than catshit."

We drove down Highway One, rather more slowly than we had come up. Greg dropped me at my car, thanked me for the lunch, and trudged up to his studio, presumably to attack the lady with the fetching behind. I pointed the Mercedes north without much enthusiasm. I was depressed. What had looked like an earth-shaking incident about to happen had very quickly become another fiasco of the imagination.

24

"Lunch!" she said.

As I DROVE up the highway toward Carmel, I unwrapped the sandwiches with my right hand without taking my eyes off the road (a tricky thing, really), and ate one ravenously. The salad at Chutney's hadn't assuaged the inner man, and the pastrami lettuce and tomatoes on dark rye helped to soothe my dampened spirits. On the other hand, I thought, the smell would remain in the car for weeks.

If Wilson, Summers and company were not plotting against the Pope, what were they doing with the paramilitary force? Planning an attack on Fort Ord? A raid on the Naval Postgraduate School?

It was probably all a product of my (and Reiko's) imagination. We had both been so long mired in the deadly routine of investigative services that we longed for something important, exciting. We were so hard up for kicks we had invented some.

We had all the ingredients: The sneaky ex-soldier, the industrial genius, some suspicious-looking thugs, a clandestine rendezvous during which a suitcase was opened and closed. Did the bag contain exotic weaponry? Or were these guys just partners in a real estate investment trust inspecting a lot of lapsed mortgages. Not bloody likely. We had one bonafide murder, I thought. I was convinced that Howard Gravesend (no matter how drunk) could not have fallen from

Jeffers' tower without having been pushed, conscious or unconscious. We had Carlos Vesper, a curious participant, sort of out of kilter with the rest. Alonzo Highbridge had come into the picture just recently, as one of Joanna Gravesend's several amours. He was also connected in some weird way with Vesper. Where did Michael Flaherty fit in? My God, I thought, he might have made this whole thing up.

I needed to talk to Reiko. When I get terribly confused and need a dash of pure reason, I talk to Reiko. She's not always right, you understand, but she has this way of pulling back and taking a problem apart. And she was very close to the action.

She was in the office when I arrived, dozing with her head on her arms in a distinctly uncharacteristic pose. I had never seen her nap in the office before. Panic siezed me for a moment. I shook her sharply.

"What the hell are you doing, Riordan?" she shouted. "I am just resting my eyes, resting my eyes. Lenny and I had lunch at the Wharf and I had two glasses of wine. Just sorta made me groggy. Did you see Greg?" She fumbled with her over-sized, black-rimmed glasses.

"Greg's not going to be any help, honey. Sure I saw him. We went over the whole Mission scene. There's no place where anybody could get a shot at the Pope. The cops tell me that they've got everything covered. I've heard that the Secret Service has inspected all the homes within sight of the landing area. It would take an air strike or an armored attack to get the job done. One guy with a rifle would be cut to pieces before he could get a round off. Or two guys with rifles. This whole thing is a pipe dream."

I walked into my office and sat down wearily in my chair. I'm not sure whether I was relieved or just let down. What could have been the pinnacle of my career in private investigation had eluded my grasp. Shit! Fifteen or twenty minutes must have passed when Reiko appeared in the doorway.

"Lunch!" she said.

"We've *had* lunch. I've had lunch and you've had lunch. What the hell is the matter with you."

"Not *us*, Riordan. *The Pope*. He's going to have lunch at the Mission. He's going to talk to some people, have a rest, and *lunch*."

I was annoyed. "He is a man, Reiko. He *eats*. He goes to the john.

He puts his pants on one leg at a time. Or does he wear pants under that outfit?"

"You're not getting it. Nobody can get a good shot at him, you say. Maybe they're not going to *shoot* him. Maybe they're ... "

"Going to poison his lunch? Ridiculous! How are they going to manage that?"

She smiled the smile of Buddha and narrowed her mysterious oriental eyes.

"It's going to be catered by the kitchen at La Hacienda in Carmel. That was in the paper last week. *Somebody* could break in and put arsenic in the lasagna. Easiest thing in the world."

She was right. Oh, not about the poisoned lasagna, but that there was another avenue to assassination.

"Let's go, Reiko-san. To La Hacienda. Faster than a speeding bullet."

All was not lost. I rushed madly to the elephant's foot umbrella stand and siezed my blackthorn stick. I grabbed Reiko by the hand and dragged her out the door and down the stairs to Alvarado Street. She complained all the way as I pulled her into traffic and nearly got us both killed by a UPS truck. The driver stuck his head out the window and made some sort of scatalogical reference. But in a few moments we were on our way over the hill to Carmel.

La Hacienda is an old hotel that has been completely renewed. It is off the beaten path somewhat, several blocks south of Ocean Avenue. There wasn't the parking squeeze you find nearer the tourist action.

Reiko and I made our way to the main kitchen. Just inside we were stopped by an attractive young female.

"And where the hell do you think you're going?" she said, with the kind of frown I might have in another time described as "cute."

"It's very important, miss. We're hoping we can head off a terrible tragedy."

"That's the first time anybody has said that about my food." The lady looked hurt. "What's this all about?"

"Please, miss, we've got to see the chef. It's a matter of life or death."

She drew herself up. "I *am* the chef, mac. What's your problem?"

All the chefs I had ever known were men in middle age, usually with some kind of facial hair, and either very thin or very, very fat. Here was a woman under thirty-five, well-groomed and attractive, no facial hair, representing herself as the chef of a major Carmel kitchen.

"*You* are the chef." It wasn't a question. It was an unbelieving affirmation. I composed myself. "Miss . . . ?"

"*Ms.* Collins. Who the hell are you?"

I made a clumsy introduction. Reiko did her Japanese bow. I extended my hand to Ms. Collins and, after a moment's hesitation, was given a vice-like handshake.

"Come into my office, Mr. Riordan, Miss Masuda." She led us through the spotless kitchen to a cubicle about six feet square, motioned us in and shut the door. There was only one chair which Chef Collins immediately occupied. Reiko and I stood there looking dumb.

"Now, what is so important?" she asked.

"You are catering the luncheon for the Pope next Thursday, right?"

"That's no secret. It was in The Herald last week. Come to the point. You know his favorite recipes?"

"We have reason to believe that there is a conspiracy to assassinate the Pope. And we have come to the conclusion that the assassins might try to get the job done with poison."

"You are, of course, out of your minds." She looked amazed and unbelieving. "That is pure bullshit. How in the world . . . ?"

"You're sure of all your people, Ms. Collins?"

"Every one. I've hired all of them myself. Unquestionable references every one."

"Take on anybody lately?"

"No. Well, yes, as a matter of fact. Two weeks ago my salad man took off without warning. I hired a man to take his place. But he couldn't be dangerous. He came directly from a private employer who entertains lavishly and has one of the best kitchens in Pebble Beach."

"What kitchen? What employer?"

"Very wealthy man. Computer money. Arthur Wilson."

25

"Learned to cook in the army."

REIKO AND I looked at each other, and she began to shuffle her feet. I needed to head off a full display of her dance of excitement which probably would have completely disrupted Ms. Collins' small office. I squeezed her arm tightly.

"Is this man here now?"

"No, as a matter of fact. But he's due very soon. He's on dinner tonight. But Frank couldn't possibly have anything to do with a terrorist plot. He's such a mild sort of fellow. Granted, he *looks* threatening, but he's really a very sweet guy. Really great with endive."

"Do you mind if we wait for him. There are some questions we'd like to ask. Nothing inflammatory. Just routine."

She looked doubtful, but she nodded and shrugged. "OK. Just don't get in the way of the help."

We took up positions near the street entrance of the kitchen, lounging against counters, trying to look inconspicuous. The dinner shift was coming on, looking sharp and professional in starched jackets and caps. In a short while a burly, crew-cut man appeared in the door, and Reiko pinched me so hard I yelled out loud. "It's one of *them*," she hissed. "One of the guys who was at Summers' house, and later at the picnic grounds. The guy who dropped his end of the suitcase."

I moved into position to intercept the newcomer. "Pardon me, sir, but we're private investigators. We need to ask you some questions about a certain matter. Is there somewhere we can go?" The man showed little alarm or surprise. He motioned to Collins' now unoccupied office, and we filed in.

I was looking for the proper opening gambit. "You were late in the employ of Mr. Arthur Wilson, is that right?"

"Yes. For more than a year. So what?" The man's eyes were beginning to show suspicion. He was big. He had a jutting jaw and eyebrows that grew together. I took a firm grip on my blackthorn stick.

"Your name is Frank? Didn't get the last name."

"Allen. Frank Allen."

"Frank, were you ever in the service?"

"Goddam right. Twelve years. Learned to cook in the Army."

I winced inwardly. An Army cook in an upscale restaurant? A Spam handler?

Exercise caution, Riordan. If this guy is as tough as he looks, you could be in for great trouble. I approached the most important question gingerly.

"Have you ever had any ... er ... *association* with a retired Lieutenant Colonel named Summers?"

It all happened in a split second. I didn't know what hit me. All of a sudden I was against the wall with a split lip and a total loss of orientation. The guy hadn't even given me a chance to block the blow with my stick. He had slugged me and burst out of the office in one big motion. Out of the corner of my eye, in my daze, I could see Reiko grab a cast-iron frying pan and take off after him. I shouted at her to stop, but I couldn't get much voice up. Wiry little lady. How did she get the wrists to handle that heavy pan? Dimly I heard a car start and lay down a lot of skid marks in a quick getaway. After what seemed to me to be an age, Reiko came back into the office in slow motion and leaned over me.

"Are you OK? Your eyes are crossed. Here, let me help you up."

I swear this little pixie female, weighing a good 85 pounds fully dressed, dragged me up off the floor and dumped me in Chef Collins' chair. I was vaguely aware that she left and returned with a cold towel that she pressed to my temples. The real world gradually returned.

"I guess he was our man, huh?" said Reiko. She wiped the blood off my lip with tender loving care. "You're losing your timing. I thought you could see a punch coming, rojin-san." Don't kick an aging man in his macho when he's down, little one. But I was grateful to have her around, no matter how many barbs she threw at me.

"He was our man. No doubt. Either that or he took me for an old enemy."

"What does that do to the plot to kill the Pope? And what do we do now?"

"Let's go back to the office. You drive."

Neither of us had much to say on our way over to Monterey. Reiko is all business when she drives. Her hands are on the wheel at the correct two-and-ten positions. Her eyes are glued to the road ahead of her. And she normally exceeds the speed limit by ten to fifteen miles an hour.

I was still pretty woozy when we got back to the office. My jaw hurt, my head ached, and my lip was still bleeding.

"Lean on me," said Reiko.

"Are you out of your mind? I am twice your size."

"Try me." I put my arm around her shoulders and, sure enough, she boosted me up the stairs to the office.

"How are you at karate, Reiko-san?"

"Lethal. My uncle began teaching me when I was six. Don't make a wrong move."

We sat for a while in my office in deep silence. I was thinking of all the crazy things that had happened since Howard Gravesend came to tell me of his impending divorce and hire me to chase Joanna. I'm not sure what Reiko was thinking, but the wheels were going around very swiftly, indeed. She broke the quiet.

"I think this Pope thing has had us off the track. I think the Wilson-Summers action is pointed in another direction. I think Howard Gravesend was murdered because of something he knew. If we could find out *what* he knew, we'd be home free. Or at least rounding third."

"You mean there was no threat on the Pope's life?"

"No. I think that was icing on the cake. A serendipity thing for Wilson. He could get the Pope as a kind of gesture. But his main move has to be in another direction."

"What direction?"

"I have no earthly idea."

"You are a hell of a lot of help."

"Look at it this way, Riordan. It didn't take Greg long to figure that an assault at the Mission was foolhardy. Summers must have seen that. The ringer at the restaurant was a last resort, but there's nothing really lost, don't you see. No, there's something else moving. And, damn it, I don't know what."

"Any idea where we go from here?"

She shook her head slowly, leaned back and put her feet up on my desk. I think she forgot for a moment about the mini skirt. I averted my eyes to avoid becoming a karate victim. Or maybe she thought I was just too old to react.

Suddenly her feet hit the floor. "There may be one other source to tap. One player hasn't been checked out yet. We ought to run over to Salinas and talk to Alonzo Highbridge."

26

"Hell, you didn't sound oriental."

I NEVER REALIZED until I accidentally looked at a map of the county that the road from Monterey to Salinas doesn't go due east in a straight line. If it did, it would just about bisect Fort Ord. The road leaves the Peninsula with good intentions, swings south and make a grand curve skirting the military post, winding up in a northeasterly direction into Salinas.

Fort Ord is where a lot of West Coast young men got their first taste of the military life in the last three wars. It's huge, big enough for an Infantry Replacement Training Center, which it was for a lot of years. Big enough to contain an artillery range. Big enough so you could get lost out there somewhere. I thought about my own days there as we drove by. God, I was young! And I wasn't really sure where Korea was.

When you go from the Monterey Peninsula over to Salinas, you're changing worlds. The Peninsula is vacationland: deep sea fishing, fine restaurants and hotels, Carmel-by-the-Sea, *movie stars*. Salinas is the county seat: the county jail, the county courthouse, the Lettuce Growers Association, the great California Rodeo. Moving from one place to the other you are exchanging L.A.-San Francisco sophistication for a genuine chunk of the Old West. It's Steinbeck country, scene of *East of Eden*, "Salad Bowl of the World." One of the guys who

119

owned the Salinas TV station, KSBW, once told me that was what the
SBW stands for.

Reiko had called Highbridge's office to see about an appointment.
He had answered the phone himself and said, "Why, hell yes, come on
over, honey. Ain't nobody in the office but me, so just come right on in
when you get here."

We pulled up in front of a drab, stucco building on a side street.
Above the front door was a stained and faded sign that said "Highbridge Produce." Nothing about the place suggested that the man
inside was probably one of the five wealthiest people in a town of
surprising affluence.

In the process of her thoroughgoing research, Reiko had done a little
background investigation on Highbridge. He had been born and
reared to adulthood in Paris, Kentucky. Part of his early training was
shoveling manure on a horse farm, a fact of which he was perhaps
inordinately proud. After service in World War II, he, like so many of
his contemporaries, became restless, and headed west for California.
He had managed to get into Stanford on the GI Bill. After graduation,
he had found a home in Salinas in the early fifties, put his farm
experience to work in the lettuce fields, and through a combination of
raw intelligence and horse sense (acquired from handling all that
manure, I think), was able to rise to the top of the heap. Like so many
auslanders, he took the West to his bosom completely. Like so many
Salinas Valley farmers, he affected western garb, including boots and
ten-gallon hat. No person of his acquaintance could remember ever
having seen him wear a business suit.

Reiko got out of the car and came around to help me. I was still not
too sure of my reflexes, so I had let her drive. She pointed me toward
the door. I was still clutching my blackthorn stick.

The door led into a hallway smelling of musty dampness, like an
old school building. There were offices ranged along the hall, a row of
doors with identical frosted glass upper halves. We walked slowly,
inspecting the legends on each door. Reiko, in the dimness, surrepti-
tiously extracted her big spectacles (which she had snatched off when
we got out of the car) from her purse and perched them on her nose.
Finally, she halted before what I presumed was the right door and
quickly stuffed the glasses back in the purse.

"This is it," she said. "It says 'A. Highbridge, Private'. He said to come on in." And she did.

We were in a typical secretary-receptionist pen with an empty desk behind a low barrier and a few chairs arranged around a low table containing ancient magazines. The room was as drab as the outside of the building had promised. Beyond the secretary's desk was a heavy oak door with "Highbridge" lettered on it in gold. Reiko walked directly to it and opened it without knocking.

" 'Bout goddam time you got here. I was just fixin' to leave. You the little lady I talked to? Hell, you didn't sound oriental."

Alonzo Highbridge was standing behind his desk, a tall, stooped man with thinning gray hair, deep-set eyes and hollow cheeks. Without the dark tan, he could have passed for a TB victim. But the spring in his step as he came around the desk to greet us belied his appearance.

I had to get the first words in before Reiko began her little routine that began with, "You are surprised I know your language, round-eyes. . . . "

"Mr. Highbridge, I am Patrick Riordan. This is my partner Reiko Masuda. We are private investigators. Well, hell, she told you that on the phone, I'm sure. We're working on some matters involving business acquaintances of yours, Arthur Wilson and Carlos Vesper. You *are* familiar with those names?"

Highbridge sat on the front of his desk and examined us with a critical gaze. He had been in many tricky situations, and he wasn't about to be intimidated. Nothing short of a posse with a rope would shake this man. He squinted as he looked at Reiko.

"Lady, I thought you told me your name was McSorley or somethin' like that." He turned to me. "Sure, I know 'em. Me and Carlos and some other fellows, we was goin' to make a move on Mr. Wilson's company over there in Monterey. Lots of people know that."

"How well do you know Vesper?"

"Well, the little shit sold me some truly bad securities, he did. But, when I was fixin' to beat him up, he come up with this stuff about Wilson's company. I've played golf with Wilson. Been to parties at his house. Don't like parties in Pebble Beach. Too many phonies. Don't like Wilson much, but that's another story."

"You don't like Wilson because he aced you out of Omicron, right?"

He was unfazed. He smiled faintly. "That ain't quite right, Mr. Riordan. I never had nothin' to do with Omicron. That was Art Wilson's baby. No, we was partners early in the game, when Art was ready to move in his old business but didn't have the capital. I had already made me a bundle down here when Art—we was roommates at Stanford, would you believe it—called and told me he needed money. We went into this partnership thing, but just when the big breakthrough was comin', he screwed me good. Still don't know how it happened. Guess I turned my back on the wrong man."

"You know Joanna Gravesend, don't you, Mr. Highbridge?"

There was a barely perceptible change in his face, a certain ruddiness invaded the tan. "You know more than I'd ordinarily want you to know, Mr. Riordan. But I guess that's Vesper's fault, too. Joanna's a ... *friend* of mine. Well, more than just a friend, as you probably are well aware. What about her?"

"Just thought you might know some of the other folks in this cast of characters that I've been investigating. And maybe, just maybe, something about the untimely death of Howard Gravesend."

"Ah, Howard. Now, that was really too bad. He was a good lawyer. Got my son off on a pretty nasty charge. I was truly grateful." The Texas drawl was beginning to fade and some of the Stanford was coming through. "Always felt a little guilty about Joanna—but it was *her* idea."

I sensed that he was just a little less sure of himself than he had been when the conversation began. He was still in control, but there was a definite change in the atmosphere.

We were still standing, Highbridge leaning against the front of his desk, Reiko and I before him at a sort of parade rest.

Reiko spoke for the first time. "Can you think of any reason for Howard to kill himself? Or can you think of anybody who had reason to murder him? Could his death have anything to do with Arthur Wilson?"

"Y'know I just remembered I got to get a haircut. You folks can find your way out, can't you?" Highbridge turned away from us and strode to a hatrack in a corner behind his desk. He clapped on a white Stetson and faced us again. His face wasn't very friendly.

I persisted. "Are you aware of Arthur Wilson's military activities? Aside from his service in WW II and Korea?"

"You know, that old barber of mine is a crusty old bastard. If you don't show up on time, he won't wait. I'm sorry."

"When was the last time you talked to Wilson? Have you seen him in recent years? Do you know Lt. Col. Edward Summers, USA, retired?"

Fire came into the eyes of the tall thin man in the cowboy hat. He took a step toward us.

"You will get the hell out of here right now, or I will kick the shit out of you, you and your little gook!"

I felt it wise to retreat. I took Reiko by the arm before her karate instincts arose, and guided her out the door, down the hall and into the street.

She was seething all the way back to Monterey. I drove this trip. The session with Highbridge had swept all the cobwebs out of my head.

Finally Reiko spoke: "There are some liars out there, Riordan. But who are they? I have come to the conclusion that some of the things other people have told us about Arthur Wilson are not true. *Or* that *everything* anybody has told us about him is suspect. *Or* that Arthur Wilson is not exactly what he seems to be. *And* I know for sure that Alonzo Highbridge is a red-necked sonofabitch!"

27

"Either you are very brave or very stupid, Riordan."

JOANNA GRAVESEND was waiting in front of my office when we got back, pacing back and forth over a litter of cigarette butts.

"Where have you been? I've been here over an hour, waiting for you."

"Please forgive us, Joanna," I said, soothingly. "We might not have got back at all, and then where would you be? We certainly didn't know you'd be waiting."

"I have not been able to get you on the phone. I am in a state of total confusion as to what to do about the hundred thousand dollars Summers wants for my manuscript. I took a chance and went up to Summers' house this morning and was met at the door by the ugliest man I've ever seen and told that 'Summers don't live here no more.' What do you know? Have you *anything* new to report to me?"

Reiko and I looked at each other. "The ball is in your court, Reiko-san," I said. She looked nervous.

"Joanna, I've done a good bit of research on Stevenson's time in Monterey. *And* his poetry. And it is my conclusion that that old manuscript is a fake. Something your great-grandfather made up himself."

The lady in the high-fashion threads and theatrical make-up sagged. I caught her around the waist and helped her through the office door.

She clung to my arm, and I could feel the thinness of her through the expensive clothes. All bones, she was. A quick thought flashed through my mind: it would be like making love to a surf-board. I settled her gently in my office client chair and turned to Reiko: "Do we have anything to drink around here? You know I don't keep booze in the office, but . . . "

My partner ducked out and returned almost immediately with an unopened bottle of Chivas Regal. "It was a gift. From George Spelvin. He always forgets that you don't drink. I've been saving it." She frowned. "It doesn't spoil, does it? It's been here since last Christmas."

"It doesn't spoil, honey. It doesn't get any better in glass, either. It just sort of lies there mellow. Get me a glass."

My hand shook just slightly as I poured the twelve-year-old Scotch into a glass. Scotch had been my favorite companion in my drinking days. I had made an honest effort to consume most of the Scotch in San Francisco in the months after my wife's death. But I hadn't had a drop of anything in the ten years since Reiko had entered my life. I took a deep breath and shook off the temptation. All I had to do was remember those many days that I *couldn't* remember.

Joanna sipped the liquor slowly. Gradually her face lost the terrible tension it had shown when we found her at the office door.

"Riordan, if that manuscript is not the real thing, I am in deep trouble. That was my last hope. The family money has run out. Howard didn't leave a dime. The insurance company has been playing games with me because they contend that Howard's death *might* have been suicide. The house in the Meadows and the small place on the Point are both mortgaged to the hilt. I didn't have any idea where I was going to get the money to ransom the manuscript unless it was from . . . a man I know in Salinas."

"Alonzo Highbridge. We just talked to him. A real old-fashioned Western character. Good ol' country boy."

"All right, so you know about my affair with Highbridge. And I guess you know about Sam Pickett and the others."

"Pickett? Is he the guard from Soledad or the insurance agent from Marina?"

"Oh, no. Sam teaches at Cabrillo College. Contemporary literature. He's quite a well known poet."

Another poet. Can we separate the good guys from the bad guys that way? The poets are the good guys and the non-poets wear the black hats?

I glanced at Reiko and she shook her head. She'd missed that one.

"I am curious, Joanna. How have you been able to handle all these men friends? Do you have a schedule? Is there a calendar stuck to your refrigerator with little magnets that look like hot dogs?"

She looked up at me with tears welling in her eyes and I felt like a cheap, insensitive bastard. "I'm sorry. Guess I've got a nasty streak that comes out now and then."

Joanna Gravesend, with tears on her flushed cheeks, looked like a young girl who had just been left at the altar. It was as if the stiff high-fashion model had just been deprived of all her starch. He mouth hung open, her shoulders drooped, she sat with her hands in her lap, tugging on a wet handkerchief. She had finished half a glass of Chivas Regal and her eyes were glazing over.

"Can I take you home, Joanna?"

She lifted her head and looked over my shoulder at a spot in the middle distance. She smiled. "Just let me sit here a while. I'll be all right."

I motioned Reiko to follow me into the outer office.

"Listen, partner, very carefully. After Joanna's had a chance to simmer down, see how much you can get out of her about Highbridge. I am convinced that he is more involved in this bloody mess than we could have suspected. Meanwhile, I'm going over to Carmel to pay a visit to Summers. If one of the thugs was there to scare off Joanna, there's a good chance that Summers is there, too. Or soon will be."

I grabbed my trusty blackthorn walking stick and set out for Carmel. It was late afternoon in September, the sun arrested high by Daylight Saving Time and still shining brightly and warmly over the Peninsula. When I arrived in the village by the sea, the tourists were swarming, and traffic was heavy. I had come down Carpenter on the truck route to Junipero and was headed south. The intersection of Junipero and Ocean is the deadliest five-way stop in all of California. Cars are streaming down Ocean from Highway One. Equally heavy east-bound traffic is trying to go through in the other direction. Into this mess comes Mountain View at a forty-five degree angle. And the traffic north and south on Junipero is trying to sneak through at the first opening. Please don't misunderstand. I love Carmel. I just wish they'd get some traffic signals. And more marked intersections. But these things would reduce the charm of the place, I guess.

After successfully negotiating the big intersection, I drove on down to Tenth Avenue and turned left. I parked the Mercedes a discreet distance from Summers' place and got out. The house is on a steep hill and I was glad I had my blackthorn stick. I have a little trouble with my knees. Old football injury, you know. I was never all that good at the game, but I *do* have "football knees."

Perhaps it was foolish. Perhaps I should have exercised more caution. But at the time the only way I could think to approach the problem was to go up and knock on the door. There was a pickup in the driveway, and I could see people moving about inside the house.

The man who opened the door was Frank Allen. He didn't seem to recognize me. Or he just didn't have any expressions other than threatening.

"You come to the wrong place. We don't want any," he said, as he started to slam the door. A voice behind him called out, "Hold it, Frank. Let the dumb bastard in."

Lt. Col. Edward Summers, USA, ret., emerged from behind the bulk of Frank Allen. He was presenting me with a welcoming grin and gesturing me into the living room.

I walked in a few steps and looked around. The room was cold and austere, sparsely furnished with drab, functional chairs and a nondescript sofa. The floor was bare, without even a throw-rug to soften the harsh thump of GI boots that Summers and his ugly platoon were wearing. There must have been a dozen of them, about an infantry squad's worth. All wore the familiar camouflage fatigues that became part of Army issue after I got out. In Korea, camouflage stuff wouldn't have helped.

All I had ever seen of Ed Summers was his head and his right arm as he handed Joanna the manuscript from his car. Seeing the man now, without his dark glasses, was a revelation. He didn't look quite so much like G. Gordon Liddy. His brows weren't so thick, his mustache lighter in color. If he had been an inch or two shorter and had not had his hair clipped close to the scalp, I would have said he looked more like Thomas E. Dewey. Or Burt Reynolds, I could go either way. What I did see in his eyes which shook me up a bit was a sort of fanatic's gleam. Then it dawned on me: Oliver North with a mustache!

"You're Riordan, aren't you? Either you are very brave or very stupid, Riordan. These men are all armed. And they are very loyal."

"Colonel Summers, I have just come to impart to you some information. The manuscript that belongs to Joanna Gravesend. It is very probably a forgery. You are not going to get the hundred grand."

"It's of no consequence. I have all the money I need. Just thought I could take the stuck-up bitch for pocket change. Is that all you came here about?"

"No, not really. This morning I had a conversation with a gentleman in Salinas named Highbridge. I was just wondering if..."

Summers signaled his men to close in on me. I looked for a quick route to the door. Two members of the squad drew sidearms. I gripped my puny blackthorn stick in the manner of Little John as he thumped Robin Hood off the footbridge. I asked myself seriously why I had come here in the first place. The grim soldiers were pushing me to the wall when the doorbell rang.

Everything stopped. I edged closer to the door. One of the gorillas opened it. A small Asian woman in a floppy hat and large, black-rimmed glasses stood on the porch clutching a clipboard. "Hello, there. I'm collecting signatures of residents on a petition to stop construction of that awful new dam. You've heard about that, haven't you.." She smiled a winsome smile and shoved the clipboard into the gut of the very surprised soldier.

"We all gave at the office," I shouted, and burst out the door. The signature solicitor and I dashed madly out to the street. There was shouting and bad language from the house, but nobody followed us.

"I thought I left you in Monterey to talk to Joanna. You know you were risking your little ass coming here." I hugged her as we stood by my car.

"She fell asleep. The booze got to her. They've got a couch next door in Lenny's place and I told them to hang on to her if she wakes up."

"Reiko..."

"Yes?"

"When did you get those glasses?"

28

"I haven't been quite straight with you, Pat."

TAKE ME TO MY CAR, Riordan. It's way up on Junipero. I didn't want to get too close."

"You're evading the issue." She had her head turned away from me. I repeated the question:

"When did you get those glasses?"

Reiko squirmed in her seat and tugged at her safety belt. She looked steadily out the window as I drove slowly up the street, even though she had seen everything a thousand times before.

At long last, with a deep breath, she turned to me.

"I have worn contact lenses since high school, Riordan. I was wearing them when I first came into your office in San Francisco. I never told you. Why should I? It was none of your damn business. It's not as if I were wearing the kind that change the color of your eyes or something. Wouldn't I look funny with blue eyes?" She smiled, weakly.

"So why now the glasses?"

She closed her eyes tight. "It's all so silly. I just don't do things like that."

"Like what?"

There was a long pause.

"I swallowed them. Not the glasses. The contacts. I felt so *dumb.*"

"Reiko, how could you swallow your contacts?" I was trying to be very gentle.

"Well, my eyes were irritated from something. Probably the junk in the air, you know. The doctor gave me some drops to use every three or four hours. The thing was, though, that I had to take the contacts out for ten minutes or so. Or the stuff in the drops would have turned them brown or something. Anyway, I got into the habit of putting the contacts under my tongue, and. . . . "

"Under your tongue?"

"Yeah. The right lens on the right side and the left one on the left. You know those little pockets under your tongue? It worked fine for a while."

"Don't you know that there are more bacteria in your mouth than in any other part of your body, Reiko-san? That was a crazy thing to do."

"I know. But I figured the medicine would sterilize the lenses. Or sterilize my eyes. Anyhow, I was sitting in the office with my lenses under my tongue and the medicine in my eyes when Lenny came in with a cup of tea. He's nice that way. Honestly, Riordan, I just didn't think. I took a sip of tea, and, whoosh, there went the lenses. I couldn't see Lenny real well, so I just smiled and thanked him. When he left, I pulled out the glasses I wear at home so I could see my keyboard. After that whenever I heard anybody coming near the office, I pulled the glasses off."

"What kind of contacts? Hard or soft?"

"Soft. I used to wear hard, but soft can stay in longer."

"Well, they certainly would navigate your alimentary canal, partner. You could. . . . "

"Don't even say it! I couldn't do that." She ducked her head and made an awful face.

"So what do you do now?"

"I'm waiting. The lenses were special. Made just for me. With an astigmatism correction. I won't get 'em for a couple of days more."

"Well, you can wear your specs around me, honey. I still think you're beautiful."

She looked at me wistfully. "You couldn't possibly know what it's like to be terribly nearsighted."

"I guess not, Reiko-san. I guess not." I put my arm around her shoulders and gave her a little hug. That was a pretty good move in my youth. All the young bucks of my generation were experts in one-hand driving, proud of being able to shift gears while undoing a bra strap. I delivered her to her car and followed her back to Monterey.

When we got back to the office the blinking light was signalling on the answering machine. I punched the button to get the calls:

"Pat, this is Tony Balestreri. I'm back in town. Paul Edwards told me about the Gravesend thing. I've read the file. Like to talk to you."

"Mr. Riordan, you were recommended to me by George Spelvin. I have a very delicate problem. It involves my only son, who apparently has left home with his psychotherapist to live in San Francisco. Could you call me as soon as possible."

"Riordan. Alden Crowley here. Need to talk. Call back."

"Friends, this is Michael Flaherty. I'm just a wee bit disturbed by something I just learned about Arthur Wilson. I'll call later."

And finally: "This is Art Wilson. I haven't been quite straight with you, Pat. There are some things we ought to discuss. Can't do it on the phone. Come see me if you can get here before five. Or first thing tomorrow morning."

This last message got to me. I had never heard Wilson sound so somber and hesitant. I looked at the clock. Quarter to five. Too late for this day. Catch him tomorrow.

Crowley and Flaherty could wait. The runaway youth could probably be traced to the Castro District in San Francisco. I returned Balestreri's call.

"Tony! What's new? How was the vacation?"

He sounded glum. "You ever take a vacation in a recreational vehicle with a bunch of kids? No, you've got no kids. And your whole life's a vacation. Enough said about that. No, Paul told me you were concerned about foul play in the death of Howard Gravesend. What I get from the file just indicates that the guy got drunk and fell off the Jeffers tower. It's a closed case. *Unless* you have any further evidence of murder."

I went back to the beginning and told the whole story in meticulous detail: the Wilson connection, the Highbridge connection, the very weird Lt. Col. Summers, Carlos Vesper, the entire enchilada.

When I finished there was a long, low whistle on the other end of the line.

"You know this sounds like you made it all up. I know there are a lot of eccentric characters around, especially on the Peninsula. But this is ridiculous, Patrick. Ridiculous."

"You are absolutely right, Sergeant."

"This thing about the Pope. You sure there isn't any danger of a real attempt being made to kill him?"

"Reasonably sure. No professional terrorist would risk making a move out at the Mission. Unless he were a religious fanatic. And we're not dealing with any of those. I'd be willing to wager that Summers' men don't go to church. They all think they're hotshot mercenaries, Tony. And Summers himself is too battle-wise to waste his troops on an unattainable objective. The business with the cook in the catering kitchen was a back-door move that might have worked, but it was not all that hard to figure. When we scotched that ploy, the Pope thing went out the window, I'm sure. But Summers' mini task-force is trained for something. Damned if I know what it is."

"Keep in touch. I'll nose around and see what I can find. What was the Salinas guy's name again?"

"Highbridge. Alonzo Highbridge. Plenty high profile in the lettuce biz."

"And the crooked stockbroker? Sounds like a Peter Lorre character."

"Carlos Vesper."

"Talk to you later, Riordan. Goodbye."

I called Reiko into my office. She appeared serene, wearing her enormous glasses. "Yes, partner?"

"How about a plate of prawns in lobster sauce at Chef Lee's? I don't know about you, but I'm getting a bit peckish. Nice Chinese dinner go good?"

"I'm sorry, Pat, but I have a dinner date."

"With Lenny?"

"Uh . . . no. Actually it's a *first* date. I'm kinda surprised to have it. But he'll have to take me *with* glasses. He's never seen me in glasses. I don't even know where we're going to eat. I've always thought of him as somebody who eats beans out of a can heated over an open fire. But, you never know."

"Who's your date, Reiko-san. Do I know him?"

She seemed hesitant and a little shy. "Sure. You've known him a lot longer than I have. Greg Farrell."

To say that I was shocked would be an understatement. The idea of Reiko going out with Greg was unthinkable. I snorted, flushed and grew wide-eyed in disbelief.

"Are you serious?"

"Couldn't be more serious. What's the matter with you? You look like you're about to have a stroke. Let me get you a glass of water."

"No. No water." I was beginning to focus better now. I took her by the hand. "Don't you know, little one, that Farrell is known as the Don Juan of the Peninsula? That every woman who has ever been in his company has fallen hopelessly in love with him? That...."

"Hold it. You're doing it again. I can take care of myself, partner. If I feel like messing around, I'll mess around. But nobody—not even Don Juan—can make me do what I don't want to do. Besides, why should you care?"

I *had* done it again. Reiko was going out to dinner with one of my best friends, and I was being overprotective, as if she were a teenager.

"Bless you. Don't stay out late. Make him pick up the check."

At that point, Farrell stuck his head into the office. "Are you ready. Has old dad said you can stay out until ten o'clock?"

"Beat it, both of you. I hope you get indigestion." To Reiko: "I'll see *you* bright and early in the morning."

After they were gone I just sat in the quiet of the office for nearly an hour. My appetite had diminished. I no longer felt like moo goo gai pan and sesame chicken. I was depressed.

The phone rang. It was Sally Morse. "Do you have a radio? You know, I've never seen one in that sloppy office of yours."

"No, Sal, I do not have a radio. Such a device is not conducive to the kind of deep thinking I have to do. Your question is incompetent, irrelevant and immaterial..."

"Riordan, you are an arrogant sonofabitch. *If* you had a radio *and* you had been listening during the past half hour, you would know that Arthur Wilson was killed this evening. A couple of thugs burst in on him with automatic weapons just after five o'clock and splattered him all over his office."

29

There was a lot of blood.

I RAN DOWN the stairs and out to my car. In ten minutes, I was heading out Garden Road towards the Omicron plant. The man I had almost convinced myself was the "bad guy" in the whole mess had been killed in his own office. Arthur Wilson was off the hook. Dead, yeah, but off the hook.

I certainly wasn't clear about what I could do at the scene of this latest crime. But I had to get there and see for myself. It was almost as if I couldn't get my mind to accept Wilson's death unless I actually saw the body.

When I got to the factory, there were three or four Monterey police cars stopped in various attitudes, their lights creating an amusement park atmosphere. An ambulance stood at the ready, its rear doors open. I slid the Mercedes into the slot it had occupied the last time I visited this place, and got out. There wasn't a lot of noise. Cops were standing around talking, curious onlookers were being restrained at a respectable distance. I approached the lighted doorway to Wilson's office.

"Back up, buddy. Sorry, no visitors. The show's over. Man's dead." A large policeman pushed me gently but firmly in the chest.

"Riordan. Private investigator." I fumbled for my ID. "I was doing some work for Mr. Wilson."

"Just cooperate, Mr. Riordan. Nothing you can do in there."

A voice came from the doorway. "Let him in. He might be helpful." I looked up and saw the FBI man, Al McManus.

The policeman let go of my shirt front reluctantly, and pushed me towards McManus.

"Come in, Riordan. Let me show you what sometimes happens to patriotic, respectable citizens who work for Uncle Sam." He led me into the plainly furnished office of Arthur Wilson. The body lay behind the desk. There was a lot of blood. There must have been a couple of hundred bullet holes in the wall. I felt sick. In the normal course of events, I don't see too many dead people. And the spectacle of Arthur Wilson's bullet-riddled body was something out of a bad gangster movie. I heard his voice on the tape again: "I haven't been quite straight with you, Pat." What had he intended to tell me? Would I ever know now?

I turned to McManus. "What is it all about? Wilson hired me. Then I find out he is working with Lt. Col. Ed Summers. Then there's a big to do about an attempt on the life of the Pope. But that has turned out to be just a half-hearted side-bet. The mission didn't have anything to do with the Mission. But there's got to be a connection here with Summers and his thugs."

Another voice came from behind me. "Too bad we couldn't tell you more, Riordan. But it was all top secret."

I turned and faced Schneider and Stramm, the Tweedle-dee and Tweedle-dum of Omicron Megabyte Systems. It was Stramm who had spoken.

"We've been looking after him, Riordan. I thought we had all the bases covered. Things had wound down for the day and we didn't expect a hit to be attempted here. Even though they tried before."

"Who tried before? I know somebody took a few shots at Wilson's car, but I thought that was just a trick to divert suspicion from Wilson, not a legitimate attempt on his life."

Stramm took my elbow and steered me to a low couch.

"We're CIA, Riordan. Schneider and I have been under cover for a solid two years as a couple of high class errand boys for Wilson so we could keep him covered."

"I don't believe you. Mike Flaherty wrote this whole thing, didn't he. Or I'm dreaming. I *know* McManus is a fed. But you guys? Let me see some ID." They moved simultaneously, as if in a drill, each nipping a neat little leather case from an inside coat pocket. It was confirmed. They were from The Company.

"Take it easy, Riordan. We're real people. A little too real, sometimes. We let this one get away from us. Listen: Two and a half years ago, our agency got wind of a movement being fronted by Colonel Summers. It was a typical underground operation. Summers was recruiting as many tough guys as he could find for a move in Central America. He was funded by a lot of well-meaning rich people who were looking for Communists under their beds every night. Despite what you may have heard, the Government frowns on that sort of activity. At least, now *this* branch of the government does. We started looking into the affair.

"Before we got very far, we found a link between Arthur Wilson and Summers. They had served together in the Reserve. They'd even founded a sort of patriotic group together. At that point, we weren't even sure about him, but we approached Wilson. When we told him of our suspicions, he agreed readily to help us. Wilson was CIA, Riordan, believe it or not, and he was a tremendous help to us."

Believe it or not. At that moment, I *didn't* believe it. What about all the things I'd heard about Wilson's financial problems? What about the man's easy access to Summers' home (with his *own* garage door opener). I stood dumbly looking first at Schneider and then at Stramm.

Stramm put a hand on my shoulder. "Sorry to have misled you, Riordan. We didn't want you in this thing at all. But Wilson insisted that hiring you and making a fuss about the takeover attempt could bring in some information as well as convince Summers and his group that Wilson was really with them. Summers isn't all that bright, you know. He has a good combat record, but he tends to be neurotic and overdramatic. And besides, he's not the brains behind his group at all. But I'm getting into classified stuff."

"What about Carlos Vesper? Is he hooked into this mess somehow?" My mouth had been hanging open, so I closed it.

"A lightweight. An opportunist. A bullshit artist. *But* connected with the right people."

The ambulance crew had bagged the body of Arthur Wilson and

had it on the gurney on the way to the ambulance. I felt a pang of remorse as the body passed, remembering that I had believed the man to be dishonest, a bigot, a terrorist, whatever.

"Thanks, guys. Thanks for all your help in plunging me into a miserable stinking mess. I don't need your intrigue. I'm just a simple ex-PFC who's trying to do a job. A paid peeping tom, a cheap snoop. I got into this thing out of loyalty when I should have been giving most of my time to important stuff: divorces, missing persons, process serving, finding witnesses for criminal lawyers, industrial espionage. I don't like murder. There are no laughs in murder."

"Hold it, Riordan. You can't bail out now. You've got a lot of data on Summers. You know his movements, his connections. We've still got to keep an eye on him. He's rehearsing his wild bunch for something big. And we have reason to suspect that he has made us as government."

"What do you want me to do? Wait around until some clown comes into my office like Sylvester Stallone, blasting everything in sight with an automatic weapon? You crazy? And it's not just me. My little. . . . my *partner* knows more than I do about Summers and his associates. I don't want her blasted!" I then told Stramm that he could perform a physically impossible act at his earliest convenience.

Schneider spoke for the first time. "Listen, Riordan, whatever is going to happen is going to happen within a week—ten days, at the outside. We need you to keep in touch. Keep on with your investigation. Your partner doesn't need to know anything about this conversation. Look, you came out here when you heard the news about Wilson. You were shocked. Tell her no more than that. But keep on working on the Summers thing."

"Wait a minute. Reiko saw Wilson go in and out of Summers' house *before* the first attempt on his life. Who pulled that little deal?"

The CIA men looked at each other. I feel now that they must have had some occult way of communicating. Maybe it's something they get in the training.

"We figure Summers didn't want to take the chance. Killing Wilson was something that had to be done as far away from the house on Torres Street as possible. Wilson told us at the time that it was a couple of Summers' thugs in that car. But he didn't let the first attempt frighten him off. Summers, you see, was still his old buddy to his face, and Wilson couldn't afford to accuse him for fear of blowing up the whole scheme. You will continue to help us, won't you, Riordan?"

I was too tired and drained to argue. I nodded my head and agreed to call Schneider or Stramm if anything should happen. Howard Gravesend's death was still a mystery. That's where I started, and that's where I meant to finish. I walked into another office and phoned Sally.

"I'm at Omicron. Wilson's dead. I'm exhausted. Any reason I can't come out to your house, lady?"

"Have you eaten?"

"No."

"I'll run over to Safeway and get a couple of big steaks. Pick up some B&R ice cream on the way. We'll pig out before we start groping each other. And, Pat. . . . "

"Yes?"

"Illegitimus non carborundum, eh? Don't let the bastards wear you down."

30

"She's a real good kisser."

I WILL NOT BORE you with an accounting of my adventures of that night. Let it be said that I picked up a quart of chocolate peanut butter ice cream and spent the evening at Sally's indulging all the senses. It was pretty fantastic, really. But I blush.

Next morning she got up before I did, letting me sleep to knit up my raveled sleave. There was a pot of coffee ready for me when I got up.

It was ten o'clock. Sally had been gone a couple of hours, I guessed. I sat at her kitchen table in my underwear, sipping the coffee and gnawing on the end of a stale baguette which I had smeared with cream cheese.

With Arthur Wilson out of the picture, nothing seemed to make any sense. Everything had pointed to his being involved in . . . what? A conspiracy to assassinate the Pope? No, that was ruled out. Somehow involved with the attempted takeover of his own company? Insane! Somehow involved in a love triangle with Joanna Gravesend and Colonel Summers? Hell no! With Joanna, the configuration would have to have a lot more angles. Had Howard Gravesend been pushed off the tower, perhaps on Wilson's orders? What was Wilson going to tell me when he got killed? That he was working for the CIA? That he really wasn't broke? That he had just purchased the controlling interest in the Los Angeles Dodgers?

I dragged myself back into the bedroom and pulled on my clothes. There must be a better, easier way to make a living, I thought. The happiest man I ever knew was a former prize fighter in San Francisco who made all the money he needed working about eight weeks a year. He had a fireworks stand in the summer and a Christmas tree lot in the winter. The rest of the year he spent playing boss dice in bars, a game at which he was extraordinarily lucky. Too late for me, though. Anyhow, I'd probably blow up the fireworks and the Christmas trees would all get the blight.

I stopped at the Safeway in the Crossroads to pick up some supplies. I have to do that when I think about it; otherwise my cupboard is bare. In the produce department I found Greg Farrell feeling papayas.

"You can put a finger right through those, my friend, if you're not careful."

He looked up, surprised. "Hi, Pat. You're the last person I expected to see here. I didn't know you cooked."

"Of course, I cook. Man cannot live by TV dinners alone. And man cannot afford Carmel restaurants very often."

I was examining his face to see if he was feeling guilty. "How was your date with Reiko last night?"

He smiled. "She's a wonderful girl, Pat. I hope you appreciate her. We had a dandy time. Dinner at a place I know in Monterey that has checkered tablecloths and the best potato pancakes in the West. Then we went to this place Reiko knows about where they were having a Looney Tunes festival. Had a ball."

I winced. All these years I had been trying to get Reiko to appreciate some of the gourmet restaurants in San Francisco and the Peninsula. And Farrell had taken her out for potato pancakes. I was not going to ask what else they ate.

"I take it you got her home reasonably early, then?"

"Oh, sure. No sweat."

The tension was growing. I was aching to find out if he had stayed overnight at Reiko's apartment. But I couldn't ask. Greg knew just what was going through my mind, though. He grinned.

"I was down home at eleven-thirty, Pat. I kissed her at the door. She's a real good kisser."

It was somewhat comforting. "Well, sure, Greg. I knew she'd be all right with you ... despite your, well, inclinations with the ladies. She. ... "

"Turn it off, my friend. I know how possessive you are about Reiko. But remember, as somebody once said, you hold the things you love with open hands. She's thirty-six years old, Pat. We're both grown-up people. I would never think of trying to get her into bed on the first date. On the other hand. ... "

"Never mind! I'll be seeing you." I waved goodbye to him and pushed my cart towards the meat department. He moved from the papayas and began poking at the mangoes.

When I had got what I thought I needed for my kitchen, I drove back home to shave, reminding myself that I'd have to get a pack of disposable razors to leave at Sally's. The house was cold and damp. I kicked up the thermostat to take off the chill. The tile underfoot throughout the ground floor of the house makes it a little clammy on foggy mornings. And, apparently, there had been some fog early on that day.

When I opened the door of my office just before noon, I was greeted by a roomful of people. Reiko was standing in a corner, talking to Tony Balestreri. Schneider and Stramm were talking to each other in another corner. Joanna Gravesend was sitting at Reiko's desk, smoking furiously. And Carlos Vesper was sitting *on* the desk, drinking coffee from a styrofoam cup that was obviously leaking.

"Did somebody call a meeting?" I asked. "There is not enough room here for all of us. Not enough oxygen. What the hell is this all about?"

Reiko spoke: "Tony has some information for you about Alonzo Highbridge. Joanna is not convinced that her great-grandfather's original Stevenson manuscript is a phony. I don't know what those two guys over there want. Oh, and Carlos wants to borrow a hundred bucks. He tried me and I referred him to you."

Everybody started talking at once and I retreated hastily to my inner sanctum. "Send 'em in one at a time, Tony first. Write Carlos a check on the office account. He's got to get his Lamborghini out of hock. But give me a couple of minutes."

I sat down at my desk and drew a deep breath. Just Sally and me and two weeks on Maui, I thought. Away from the crowd, away from the tears and strife. Away from ugly rental soldiers carrying ugly automatic weapons. I yelled through the partition: "OK! Now!"

Balestreri came through the door and sat down immediately in my one guest chair. "Do you know I have been waiting here for you on my feet for more than an hour? I'm a mobile cop. I'm not used to just standing."

"So what is it, Tony?"

"First, we think you're right about Gravesend. He had to have been pushed or thrown from the tower. If he had simply toppled, he wouldn't have made contact with the fence."

"That's gratifying. But I choose not to congratulate myself. What else?"

"The whole thing about Arthur Wilson being broke was so much bullshit. He and those two spooks made it up and spread it around to see what would come out of the woodwork. Wilson made sure Vesper would get the information. He knew Vesper had been in contact with Summers. It would tend to justify his throwing in with Summers so that he could get closer to what was happening. He also knew it would be tempting to his old business associate, Alonzo Highbridge. Obviously, Highbridge carried a grudge. Also, we think he is the brains behind Summers and his crew."

"Wait a minute. What the hell is Summers up to? Some sort of shenanigans in Central America?"

Balestreri sat back. "You'll never believe this. Summers and all of his recruits are Viet Nam vets. Every one of them is convinced that the greatest danger to the western world is the influx of Asians into the United States. There's an important meeting next week of highly placed representatives of Asian nations. At the Defense Language Institute. The spooks think Summers' boys are going to make a move on *them*. And I am pretty goddam sure that the money backing the move has come from Alonzo Highbridge, who is known to be a white supremacist of the worst order. He is suspected of having hired goons to pose as fishermen to run the Vietnamese out of Monterey Bay. What a coup it would be if he could take out a dozen or so important Asian leaders."

"What are they coming here for? Why the Defense Language Institute?"

"It's a cooperative effort to help the Southeast Asians who have settled in the States, Pat. Their greatest problem is absorbing the language. They're smart and industrious, and so are their kids. Great in math and science, where language isn't all that important. But they're having a struggle with fluency in a language that's so drastically different from theirs." .

"And guys like Highbridge want to get rid of them altogether. I'm beginning to understand his reaction to Reiko. So, what do we do? Or, better, what do *you* do?"

Balestreri chewed his mustache. "That's a sort of problem. We've been trying—the Sheriff's office and the Salinas police—to get to Highbridge to question him. Nobody can find him."

31

"I've found your guerrilla warriors, Pat."

LET ME GET this straight, Tony. You think that Alonzo High-bridge is the Professor Moriarty of this complicated situation. And he's missing. Where have you looked?"

"His office, his home. Some known hangouts. For all his money, the guy likes really raunchy saloons. Everybody knows him, but nobody's seen him. Or will admit having seen him."

"How about Carmel? How about Summers' place?"

"Empty. Carmel police have it covered. Twenty-four hour surveillance. Nobody's been near it since they went in with a search warrant."

"Maybe Highbridge and Summers and their friends are ready to make their move."

"Not really. The meeting is scheduled for next Wednesday."

"Maybe they're all camped somewhere. Back in the woods, practicing their maneuvers, shooting at targets, toasting marshmallows."

"Be serious, Pat. These guys may be just a little bit crazy but they mean business. There's no doubt in my mind that they're going to mount an attack on that meeting."

"Are you covering the meeting? Who's got the jurisdiction."

"Federal property. We've alerted them. They've arranged to post a guard when the delegates arrive."

"So what do *we* do?"

Balestreri paused deliberately and checked out his fingernails. "We'll keep looking for Highbridge and Summers, and hope for the best. Come next Wednesday, there's likely to be a pitched battle around the Defense Language Institute."

"Keep me posted," I said as Balestreri rose and made for the door. "If there's going to be gunplay, I'll stay away."

As Tony was going out the door, Carlos Vesper poked his head in. "Just wanted to thank you, Riordan. I'll make it up to you. You'll see." He waved the check Reiko had given him. "I've got some inside information. You'll get your money back and a lot more." Of course, that was the middle of September of 1987. (Vesper was last seen around here on the twentieth of October of that memorable year, wearing dark glasses and boarding a Greyhound bus. I have often wondered what he thought he could do with my hundred bucks.)

Schneider and Stramm tried to come through the door simultaneously, a piece of business from a lot of old Laurel and Hardy shorts. Stramm, the rumpled one, did all the talking.

"Riordan, we think you know more than you're telling us. Who the hell was that guy Gravesend, and what do you think he had to do with this case?"

"Did you guys take a number? Howard Gravesend was a client of mine. I don't know what his connection was with Summers, or Highbridge, or anybody else, and if I did, I wouldn't tell you because it's a matter of confidentiality." I lied a little. The puzzle of Howard's death was still bothering me, and I didn't see that it was important that they should know about his defense of Highbridge's son.

"There *is* no confidentiality where the CIA is concerned, " said Stramm. He paused a beat and considered what he had said. "I mean . . . we have ways of getting the information." His face twisted. He knew he was sounding like an SS interrogator in a World War II movie, but he couldn't help himself. He broke into a wide, humorless grin. "You understand, Riordan. We're just trying to get all the facts. This is a very serious situation."

I got up and guided them to the door. "Sure, fellows, I'll keep in touch. Don't worry. We're on the same side."

My last visitor was the lovely, stylish Joanna, she of the haute couture and flat chest. She was still smoking when she came into my office.

"Joanna, please put that damned thing out. You are screwing up my sinuses."

Meekly, she stubbed out her cigarette ... on my desk top. She sat demurely and crossed her legs. Somehow she seemed thinner, more hollow-cheeked than ever.

"I know my great-grandfather's Stevenson manuscript is probably a fake, Riordan. But I want it back. For sentimental reasons. You've got to get it from that awful man."

"Wait a minute, Joanna. I don't know if the bastard still has it. And why the change of heart? I thought you were just interested in the money."

She took on a conspiratorial look. Leaning forward, she whispered hoarsely: "Flaherty doesn't know it's a fake. And he still wants to buy it. And you can't tell him it's a fake because you work for *me*." She sat upright and recrossed her legs, showing quite a bit of thigh.

Well, now, she had me. Privileged information, yet. Well, Michael Flaherty had lots of money ... and he'd probably never know the difference. He'd put that manuscript under glass in his living room, and live happily ever after.

I agreed to continue searching for the manuscript. It was probably somewhere in Summers' house, or had been used to start a fire. Joanna seemed satisfied, gave me a perfunctory kiss on the cheek, and left.

Reiko appeared at the door. "It's Greg. On the phone. He wants to talk to *you*." She looked hurt.

I picked up the phone. Farrell's voice sounded tense. He *never* sounded tense. Something was up.

"What is it, Greg?"

"I've found your guerilla warriors, Pat. They're camped way back at the end of Palo Colorado canyon. There's about a dozen of them, plus a couple of honchos. And they're loaded for bear."

32

"I didn't come all this way to sit in the car, like grandma at the picnic."

W HERE ARE YOU, Greg?" I could feel the adrenalin start to flow. Confirmed pacifist that I am, I still can remember the excitement of combat.

"At a friend's house. Right at Palo Colorado Road and Highway One. The bad guys are all the way at the end of Palo Colorado canyon. They're using the Boy Scout camp on Pico Blanco, for God's sake. I guess there won't be any kids up there for a while, and these bozos are just squatting there."

"Stay where you are. I'll be down there within the hour with reinforcements."

Happily, Tony Balestreri had stopped to flirt with Reiko and he was still hanging around when Greg's call came. I quickly informed him of what was coming down, and he made a call to assemble as many bodies as he could from the Sheriff's office. He then alerted the people at the Defense Language Institute and they promised assistance—if it was available. They said they'd have to call Ord. I had Reiko call the Omicron office and leave word for Schneider and Stramm. I grabbed my blackthorn stick, although God knows it is a puny weapon against

Uzis and shotguns. I had sworn off firearms. But I'd be prepared for hand-to-hand.

"OK," I said to Balestreri and Reiko, assuming the manner and mien of a true leader, "we're moving out." Then I thought better of it. "No. Reiko, you stay here. Mind the fort. Answer the phone. Do those things that you do so well."

"Bullshit! If you think you're leaving me behind, you're out of your gourd. I've got a right to see how this thing winds up. That sonofabitch Highbridge wants to get rid of all the people who look like me, and I want to see him hanged. Banzai!"

We piled into Tony Balestreri's patrol car for the ride down Highway One to Palo Colorado Canyon. Up to that moment, I had not realized that back seats of prowl cars are made deliberately uncomfortable to keep prisoners from getting violent. The seat is as hard as the benches in old Kezar Stadium, and it's so cramped that your knees touch and you can't straighten out your legs. This is how I rode the fifteen miles or so down the coast.

Greg was waiting for us, standing at the mouth of the canyon, where the road begins. Palo Colorado canyon is dotted on both sides with houses, most of which used to be vacation retreats but have been modernized and are now used as year 'round homes. They stretch up the road for several miles. It's a risky place to live, though. Fire insurance costs are prohibitive, *if* you can get fire insurance. And the place shares the problem of any colony along Highway One south of Carmel: the traffic is so thick at times that the poor guy who has suffered an injury (or, God forbid, a heart attack) could grow a beard—or die—before the ambulance could get him to the hospital.

Farrell peered up the road, frowning.

"Anybody else coming? I don't see how the four of us can storm the camp. You still carrying that knobby black stick, Pat. Haven't you learned anything? It's almost got you killed a couple of times."

"I told you I wasn't going to make any more holes in any more people," I snapped, not all that sure of myself. "I made a lot of holes in combat, and there were guys trying to make holes in me. This is a traditional Irish weapon, and I believe in it."

As we talked, two white cars with broad green stripes rolled up, one from each direction—Balestreri's backup Sheriff's deputies. And before he could brief them, a pair of olive drab trucks loaded with armed and helmeted soldiers came thundering down from the north. A young, wiry lieutenant jumped out of the lead truck and joined us.

"Lieutenant Andrew Berman," he announced with a snappy salute. "I'm supposed to report to a Sergeant Tony Balestreri. Is one of you him?" he said, ungrammatically, looking straight at Reiko.

Balestreri identified himself and took the Lieutenant aside to brief him on the situation. Greg put his arm around my shoulders and led me a few feet away. He had a GI forty-five on his hip and was carrying a sawed-off shotgun.

"You look pretty warlike for a guy who paints women's bare asses," I said.

"Pat, one more time. I've got some real good weapons at the house. It's just a hop and a skip away. Let me get you a little automatic or something. Just in case."

It was tempting. I had never before been confronted with a situation in which I knew there would be gunfire—since Korea, that is.

I was resolute. "Don't worry, Greg. I'll try to stay out of the line of fire. But if one of the bastards gets near me, I can knock his brains out."

Balestreri and Berman had apparently made their plans. Tony walked over to us as the Lieutenant moved briskly back to his truck. "We're going to lead," he said. "Farrell, you sit up front with me. Reiko, better go with Deputy Hubbard in that car over there. Pat, stay with us. You've got plenty of padding on your butt to ride in the back."

The convoy moved out. Palo Colorado Road runs about eight narrow, twisting miles along Bixby Creek until it ends just across the Little Sur River. The Scout camp has been there for years, a beautiful spot, wooded and silent except for the noises kids make when they're turned loose with nature. But in September, there's not much activity. Summers and his bunch must have checked it out thoroughly. It's a cinch they wouldn't have wanted a lot of adolescents barging into their maneuvers.

Householders along the way watched our procession with open-mouthed curiosity. They were used to an occasional Sheriff's car. But a couple of truckloads of soldiers—I imagine one or two of them thought we had been invaded. We didn't stop to try to explain.

When we got near the Little Sur, Balestreri pulled over and waved to the convoy to follow suit. I was grateful to be able to get out of that cramped back seat. Despite what Balestreri had said about my padding, my coccyx had been trying to poke a hole in my flesh. We gathered in a little group near the edge of the road.

"One thing first," said Balestreri. He turned to Greg. "What were you doing up here in the first place. I know where you live. Why were you wandering around miles from your house?"

Farrell had this saintly look on his face. "I ran dry, Sergeant. I was painting a series of female buns. From all angles, you know. I'm sort of an ass man, I guess. But I ran out of gas. When that happens, I always go for a hike until the spirit moves me again. Gets the blood circulating. Good for the lungs."

"Did you expect to find any bareass women on this mountain?"

"You don't understand. The things I paint are in my mind. The mind—the soul—needs regenerating. I know now what I'm going to paint next."

"I've got to ask. What?"

"Sunsets. It came to me on the way down the road today. Sunsets. It'll be a great series." He looked dreamy.

Balestreri looked unconvinced, but he made himself return to the important business at hand.

"Well, now, we've got to be very careful. The deputies and I will take the point. Lieutenant, tell your men to be as quiet as possible and follow us in two columns. Riordan, you and Reiko stay with the cars."

"Oh, no, Sergeant. I am going along on this operation. I am an ex-PFC of infantry. No way are you going to leave me behind." I really meant it. It was a matter of pride.

Balestreri lost patience. "You are unarmed, you dumb bastard. You would just get in the way."

"Forget it. I'm with you." I was adamant.

"Me, too." That was Reiko, drawing herself up to her full five feet. "I didn't come all this way to sit in the car, like grandma at the picnic." I wasn't sure what the simile meant, but I could see she was determined.

Balestreri shrugged and sighed. "Let these guys be witness to the fact that I told you to stay behind. I'm not going to have your blood on my hands."

Now, that sent a bit of a chill through me. I began to have some misgivings, but there was no turning back now. I had made my stand. On the other hand, Reiko was even more fired up.

The Sheriff's men began to move up the road, then the two columns of troops, then Reiko and me. In a few minutes we could hear voices, and Balestreri motioned the columns off the road and into the woods. This part of the Ventana Wilderness is pretty wild. A man could hide out here with ease. But a noisy squad of mercenaries was easy to find.

I could see Balestreri and Berman holding a whispered conference up ahead. Then the two columns of soldiers began to move to the left and to the right in a move to surround the camp. The voices got louder and there were shouts. Somebody in the camp had sensed our intrusion, and was giving the alarm.

The fire fight began. I don't know how many rounds of ammunition were used up, but it's a miracle nobody—I said *nobody*—got hurt. It was like one of those TV cop shows, bullets whistling everywhere and not hitting anything. But it scared the hell out of me. I grabbed Reiko and dragged her behind a big tree.

The exchange of fire couldn't have lasted longer than ten minutes or so. But it seemed forever. Finally, the sound of the guns thinned out, and I heard voices again. I took my life in my hands and peered out from behind my tree. There was smoke and the smell of gunpowder. I could see movement through the forest ahead. Suddenly, from my extreme right out of a clump of bushes, a man emerged, carrying a submachine gun. He wore a suit of camouflage fatigues and a billed cap with a silver eagle on it. He didn't see Reiko and me.

The man was trying to circle around and come up on our guys from the rear. I watched him move, carefully keeping the tree between him and the two of us. He moved stealthily, in a crouch, and I could see the concentration in his eyes. He was coming perilously near our tree. He was very nearly upon us.

We played a dangerous game of ring around a rosy, very slowly, deliberately. His eyes were fixed on the grove of trees up ahead where the fighting had been. When he passed within two feet of me, I took one step forward and brought my blackthorn stick down on his head with all my might.

He dropped like a shot, his weapon firing five or six rounds into the ground. I walked gingerly up to him and picked up the gun. The heat of it burned my hands and I threw the thing twenty feet. Then I knelt down and rolled the man over. I hadn't recognized him without his cowboy hat.

It was Alonzo Highbridge, the lettuce king, lover of wealth and women, master of all he surveyed.

33

"Then where the hell is Summers?"

I WAS STANDING over the supine body of Alonzo Highbridge, wondering if I had killed him. A trickle of blood had started down his left temple. In a second or two he groaned, and I breathed a small sigh of relief.

Tony Balestreri emerged from the clump of trees up ahead. Behind him came Summers' squad of mercenaries, their hands in the air, sheepish looks on their faces. Behind *them* came the Army troops, grinning and exchanging high-fives like the 49ers after a touchdown.

Balestreri had this silly look on his face as he approached. "What happened, Pat. Did he stumble on a rock and hit his head? Did he get struck by lightning? Did Reiko use karate on him?"

That injured my pride. "I told you that I was armed with a traditional Irish weapon. The shillelagh is but a shorter version of the blackthorn walking stick. It was named after the ancient Forest of Shillelagh, and. . . ."

"Never mind, for God's sake. Who is this guy?"

"Highbridge. I hate to admit it, but you were right."

"Then where the hell is Summers? These guys say he *was* here, but he disappeared when the shooting started. That sounds a little strange, doesn't it?"

153

Reiko piped up: "I don't think so. I think he's a big phony, from scratch. I've known men like that. One hundred per cent macho until the crunch comes. Can't get it up in a crisis. . . . "

I cut her off.

"Please, Reiko-san, don't go into a lot of details. It's embarrassing. But I think you're right about Lieutenant Colonel Summers, USA, ret. I'm also wondering about all that hero stuff he's supposed to have pulled off in Viet Nam. What do we do now, Tony?"

Balestreri shouted to Lieutenant Berman. "Get the bad guys in the truck. Leave three or four troops to watch 'em, and let's spread out and search the area for the one that took off." He looked at me. "Would you like to join us, hero? Bring your deadly stick and stay a couple of paces behind me. And the lady can come, too."

Two of Berman's soldiers had come to attend to Highbridge who was now sitting with his back against a tree, holding his head. He moaned softly, and looked at his hands, stained with his own blood.

"The bastard ran out, did he. I figured he might. Never really trusted him after he had his hair clipped and grew a mustache, trying to look like G. Gordon Liddy." He opened his eyes for the first time since I hit him. "Oh, shit, not *you!* And your little slanty-eyed girl friend."

Reiko was just near enough to catch him in the kidney with the point of a toe. It was a lightning blow, and Highbridge let out a yelp that might have been heard in Monterey.

She smiled. "That won't hurt him a bit. Oh, I mean, it *will* hurt him, but it won't do him any real damage, y'know." She was very satisfied with herself.

The two astonished GI's looked at each other, and then picked up the groaning Highbridge and carried him to one of the trucks. The rest of the troops had fanned out ready to comb the countryside for Summers.

We moved out in a wide semicircle, with Balestreri in the center, followed closely by Reiko and me. But before we had gone a hundred feet, we heard the unmistakable report of a shotgun. "Off to the left, there," shouted Lieutenant Berman.

Everybody broke into a trot and headed in the direction of the shot. Not far from the scene of the fire fight we burst into a clearing. Lying spread-eagled on the ground with a huge wound dead center in his chest was Lt. Col. Ed Summers. Thirty feet ahead of him was a smoking shotgun rigged to a frame and hooked up to a trip wire that ran through an ingenious system of metal loops to the point where it had been stumbled on by Summers. Beyond the shotgun trap was a flourishing field of marijuana.

Balestreri stood with his hands on his hips. "I should have known. These weed fields are scattered all through these hills. And the people who farm 'em are deadly folk, indeed. Even the Sheriff's people come up here in twos and threes. Looks like Summers got his in a most unheroic fashion, stumbling on somebody's dope farm."

Reiko had quietly moved away and was throwing up behind a tree. My partner is not as tough as she thinks she is. I pretended not to notice.

"Where does that leave us? Looks like all the people we believed to be bad guys are either in custody or dead. What about Howard Gravesend? Howard's death got me into this thing. And that's the one thing that's still up in the air." I guess I looked pretty confused. Balestreri either didn't hear me or chose not to notice.

"Better go help your little friend, Riordan," he said, turning to the immediate task of organizing his troops and Berman's small army. I heard him direct the soldiers to the county jail in Salinas. There was a brief discussion about who had the jurisdiction, the County of Monterey or the federal government. It was agreed that jail should be the first stop, and they could work it out from there.

All the while I felt this growing sense of failure. That's pretty silly, I guess. We *had* eliminated a lot of the garbage. The attack on the Defense Language Institute had been aborted. The truly weird plot against the Pope had been nipped in the bud. But the death of Howard Gravesend—murder or suicide or accident—was still an unsolved mystery.

I walked towards the tree that was sheltering Reiko from embarrassment. As I neared it, she appeared, eyes cast downward, pressing a tissue to her mouth. I put my arm around her and walked her to one of the Sheriff's cars.

"I'll have Norman here take you back to Monterey, Riordan," said Balestreri. "The rest of this convoy has to go in to Salinas to check these toy soldiers into the jail." He pointed to a tall young deputy with a scraggly mustache.

I helped Reiko into the passenger seat in the patrol car, and settled my badly worn butt on the hard back seat again, willing to suffer for another thirty minutes back into town. Norman uttered not a word all the way to Monterey. He nodded and almost smiled when we thanked him for the ride.

Reiko leaned heavily on me as I half-dragged her up the steps to the office. It seemed that all the starch had gone out of her. It was pretty clear that she'd never before seen a fresh corpse with a big hole in it before. A lot of people react that way. Maybe I did too, 'way back in '52 or '53, I can't remember. I *do* remember that I saw an awful lot of corpses, many of which had been my friends. And it got so I scarcely gave 'em a glance.

I made a pot of coffee. Reiko sat silently a long while at her desk. She almost never drank coffee, but when I poured her a cup, she took it in both hands and drank it almost eagerly.

"You're sort of in shock, aren't you little one?"

She looked up at me. "I didn't like him. I didn't even *know* him. But I hated to see him dead like that. All that blood. . . . "

Tears welled up in her eyes. I knelt down in front of her and took her hands. She put her head on my shoulder and cried softly for five or six minutes . . . or until my knees couldn't take it any longer.

When I got up creaking, it broke the spell. Reiko mopped her face with a handful of tissues and popped up out of the chair. "OK, what do we do next? Joanna wants that phony manuscript. Let's get out of here and find the bloody thing."

34

"H'lo, Riordan.
You know I can explain this."

THE MERCEDES had a ticket on the windshield, as usual. I plucked it off and stuffed it into my pants pocket where it would remain, probably, until the cleaner pinned it to my bill. It was growing dark and threatening rain as we pulled up in front of Summers' house in Carmel.

For the first time there was no need to park a quarter of a mile away, or for stealth as we approached the front door. The place was dark and silent, a dying house. The big trees that surrounded it probably kept the sun away even on bright days. I remembered the story about how Joanna used to take her semi-nude sun baths during those short periods when there was some ultra-violet on the soggy deck.

I pulled out a set of lock picks inherited from Al Jennings, my father's old friend, who got me into the private snoop business. "Wait a minute," said Reiko.

She made a show of rubbing her hands together and cracking her knuckles, making little Japanese sounds in her throat. Then she reached out, turned the doorknob and opened the door.

"You got to have the right technique, partner. These doors can be tricky."

The house was cold. Summers had evidently remembered to turn
the thermostat down, even though he had forgotten to lock the door. I
found the light switch. The place didn't look much more inviting than
it had appeared in the dimness of the late afternoon.

It was a typical Carmel layout. To make the best of a steeply sloping
lot, the builder had designed the house to front on the street level and
run in a straight line to the back of the lot over a deep ravine. It was
almost like an apartment in New York: five rooms in a row, ending in a
small bedroom. We entered into the living room (where I had been
rescued by Reiko from certain serious injury only a few days before), and
I again observed the Spartan nature of the furniture. The only thing that
didn't fit in with the austerity of the room was a large and expensive
stereo outfit against the far wall, dominating the room. I couldn't resist
taking a quick scan of the neatly filed tapes, mostly Wagnerian operas.
I looked around for swastikas or portraits of Hitler. But the only wall
decoration was a framed still of Robert Duvall from *Apocalypse Now.*

Reiko called from down the hall. "You've got to see this, Riordan." I
punched up the stereo and was only mildly surprised to hear elevator
music: "Kostalanetz plays Jerome Kern" or some such thing. Well, we all
have moods.

Reiko was in a small room next to the kitchen. That is, she was as far
in as she could get, and you know that she is not a big person. The room
was a survivalist's idea of heaven. It was crammed full of cartons of dried
foods and jugs of bottled water. There was enough stuff to feed a platoon
for six months.

"That ain't all, partner." Reiko took my hand and led me into the next
room which was considerably larger. On the walls all the way around
was one of the most stunning weapons collections I had ever seen. You
name it, it was there. Wooden cases, obviously containing more guns
and ammunition took up most of the floor space.

"If the Russians ever attacked Carmel, these guys were ready. Unless
Clint could hold the line at Monte Verde Street." She assumed her
karate stance. "Or maybe I'd stop 'em at Saks in the Plaza."

"We'd better get to business, Reiko-san. You go to the end of the hall
and work back. I'll start in the living room and meet you half way."

"Right, partner," she said in a bored tone. "Don't forget to look under
the furniture and in the wastebaskets."

I went back to the living room where the stereo was playing "Smoke Gets in Your Eyes." Systematically, I went through the room looking for places where a manuscript could be hidden, or perhaps discarded. There were no drawers in this room. Not a piece of furniture that contained a drawer. The stereo library was all out in the open, and the coffee table was just one big slab of glass.

I moved down the hall to the kitchen. The cabinets seemed to contain only coffee mugs. The small cupboard was crammed with soda crackers and sardine tins. The refrigerator contained large jugs of carrot juice and three cans in a six-pack of light beer. The oversized freezer compartment was stacked with TV dinners. Nothing in the garbage can under the sink but wrappers from forty or fifty Snickers bars. I felt right at home there. But no manuscript.

In the room that contained all the survival provisions there was a closet. After I strained my back moving cartons out of the way, I discovered that it was completely empty. Muttering, I moved to the gun room. Thank God, there was no possible hiding place there. Unless Summers had stuffed the manuscript into one of the weapons cases and nailed it shut. Not likely. I moved on. It was beginning to look like a fruitless search when Reiko let out a yelp from the back of the house. I dashed back to her aid, narrowly avoiding a serious fall over a rowing machine that had been left in the hall.

I entered what you might call the master bedroom. Reiko was standing at the door of the bathroom staring into it with open mouth. Inside the room, sitting on the john, clutching a large brown envelope, was Michael Flaherty.

He smiled broadly but uncertainly when I appeared over Reiko's shoulder. "H'lo, Riordan. You know I can explain this."

"I'm sure you can, Mike. But you gave the little lady here quite a start. Here now, let me guess: You figured the Stevenson poetry thing which you coveted was still here. You prowled around the house until you were satisfied that there was nobody in it, then you came on in and started looking. Where was it, anyhow?"

"Pretty cleverly hidden, I might say. But you know what a genius I am at plotting. I just said to myself, 'Flaherty, if you were a manuscript, where would you be?' Haw, haw, haw."

"So, where?"

"In the fridge, Riordan. In the freezing compartment. I haven't had a chance to look at it because it hasn't thawed out yet." His face suddenly lost its confident look, and he aged ten years in a split second. "I hope it's worth what I have gone through to get it. I'll pay Joanna for it, of course."

Reiko extended her hand to the man. "You can come out of the bathroom now. Come out and sit down on something more comfortable. I'm afraid I have some bad news for you."

Flaherty emerged, still clutching the frozen manuscript to his chest. His great beard and tangled mop of hair looked dull and unwashed. In the light of the larger room his face looked pale, except for the large red nose. He appeared anxious. Reiko steered him to the only piece of furniture in the room, a king-sized bed.

"Sit down, Michael. Now, listen: It is most probable that that manuscript is just junk, something that Joanna's great-grandfather made up himself. It's likely that Stevenson didn't write that much poetry, and what he did write was a hell of a lot better than this. I'm pretty sure. I did a lot of research."

Flaherty's face sagged even further. He seemed to shrink a couple of sizes. The brown envelope slid to his lap and then to the floor.

"After all I went through. And poor Howard. After what happened to him."

"Howard? Howard Gravesend? What are you talking about?"

The successful author of complicated suspense novels sat forward, his hands clasped between his knees. He rocked slightly as he spoke.

"I never thought I'd have to tell the tale. Oh, it was always in my mind for inclusion in a book. I try to collect all sorts of unusual things for my books, you know. But it was so strange. And we were both a little drunk."

"Go on, Michael." Reiko had assumed the position she enjoys on her tatami mat, knees on the small throw rug next to the bed, compact little bottom on her heels. I leaned against the wall and slid down to sit on the floor.

"When Joanna first told me about the existence of the Stevenson manuscript, I got this awful craving, this terrible fever. I knew I had to have it. I offered her money for it several times. But she wouldn't budge. I thought I could wear her down over a period of time. But early this past summer she decided she didn't care much for me anymore. I saw my last chance for the poetry go out the window. So I got hold of Howard. We hit it off. Howard was my kind of guy. He liked a party. He liked booze. He was a bit of a phony, just like me.

"Howard got this idea. He would go to you and give you a story about Joanna divorcing him—that part of it was true, of course—and tell you a tale about a fortune being left to him by his uncle in the Bahamas. That part I made up. Pretty clever, don't you think?" He gave us an entirely inappropriate smirk. Reiko shook her head slowly from side to side.

Flaherty looked disappointed. He continued, the smirk having vanished: "We thought that if we got you on the case, checking out Joanna's movements, that just maybe she'd eventually tell you about the manuscript. You would, then, inform Howard of it—although, of course, he already knew about it. And somehow we'd be able to get hold of it. I'd pay Howard. He always needed money." He paused for a long moment. His face was blank. "Now it sounds like it all came out of a bottle. Which it probably did." A dramatic sigh. "Anyhow, after he talked to you, he called me. He had moved out of the Carmel Meadows house a year or so ago into the little one he and Joanna had on the Point. I walked out to see him and we had a sort of celebration. I'm not sure now what we were celebrating. We had quite a bit to drink, but we weren't all that drunk. One thing led to another and we dared each other to sneak over to Tor House and climb the tower. I don't know how we did it without waking somebody, but we did. We got over the wall with no sweat. We had both been in the tower before, so we had no trouble making it to the top. We stayed up there, swaying in the wind, for maybe twenty minutes, imagining we were searching the horizon for invasion forces. Then something happened, I'm not sure what. We were on our way down. I was going first. I turned to say something to Howard and I saw him bearing down on me with both hands. He had this wild look on his face. In an instant I guessed that he was going to push me off the tower. I reacted quickly and wrenched *him* over the side. I watched him fall, and heard his head hit the wall. When I reached him, I knew he was dead. Didn't need to check the pulse. I've written about a lot of dead bodies. I can recognize dead. I guess he had been meaning to kill *me* all along."

I had no doubt that Flaherty was telling the truth. He raised his shaggy head and looked directly at Reiko, then at me. "What happened then, Michael?" Reiko's voice was gentle.

He continued in a monotone: "I panicked. I went over the wall to the street and ran all the way home. It's a wonder I didn't have a heart attack." He thumped his chest dramatically. "Rusty old pump. You know all the rest. I couldn't get the Stevenson manuscript out of my mind. That's why we chose Jeffers' tower to celebrate. You know how I feel about Jeffers. You know what a lousy poet I am. I am also a lousy human being. I guess Howard knew that. I guess he hated my guts all along." A large tear ran down each cheek. Flaherty whipped out a large red paisley handkerchief and buried his face in it.

Carmel is a place for poets, even *bad* poets. But I think I had met enough of them during those weeks since Gravesend came into my office with the crazy tale about a long lost uncle. Flaherty was still sniffling when we dropped him off at his house on San Antonio Street.

35

"Now I've got you, I'll never let you go."

NEXT DAY, I was sitting in my office, trying in vain to remember all of the details of the adventure of the lawyer who went off the tower. Sounds like a Sherlock Holmes story, doesn't it: "The Strange Case of the Vertiginous Barrister," or something like that.

Reiko was at her desk, toying with her computer. Both of us had been silent for nearly two hours, each lost in thought. I got lonely.

"Hey, partner. Can you spare a few minutes for a little conversation?"

She appeared in my doorway, wearing a charming mini-dress that I hadn't seen before. Her hair was done in a new and becoming way, and I fell in love with her again. I do that maybe once or twice a week.

"Why the fancy threads, Reiko-san? Special occasion? Celebration of our having survived the ordeal of Palo Colorado Canyon?"

She blushed just a little. "Lunch date. You don't think I'm *overdressed*, do you?"

"Au contraire, small one. You look smashing. Who you eatin' with? Lenny?"

She brushed right by that. "I am exhausted. I'm not really sure that I want this partnership after all. If it's going to be so terribly frustrating and confusing. Maybe I'd just better be a secretary and a bookkeeper and whatever. Maybe I'm not cut out to be a private investigator."

"Negative. You are a first class operative. Now I've got you, I'll never let you go."

That appeared to make her feel better. She sat down. "What happens to all these people now, Riordan? The ones left alive, I mean."

"Well, Highbridge will probably have to answer to the feds. Same for his little group. I have a notion that Flaherty will never be indicted once he's told his tale of how Howard Gravesend died. Self defense, you know. I believe his story, and I think the DA will also. Joanna will manage to live, somehow. After all she's got that poet up at Cabrillo College. Carlos Vesper may never be seen again in these parts. Or he might roll down Alvarado Street any minute in a brand new Lamborghini. Schneider and Stramm—you know, the CIA guys who were working for Arthur Wilson—they'll go back to the Company and reappear somewhere in the Middle East. Who else?"

"I guess that's about it. How about the mysterious Stevenson manuscript that I spent so much time on?"

"Oh, that. Flaherty left it with me to return to Joanna. It was still a little frozen. I haven't looked at it since it thawed out. It's on that little table by the heater."

She got up and walked to the table. She picked up the brown envelope and balanced it on her palm, as if she were trying to guess its weight.

"Is it all right to look inside?"

"Sure, honey. It isn't sealed. And it's likely to be worthless."

She fumbled with the metal clasp, and withdrew a yellowing sheaf of papers. I could see from where I sat that the writing on the pages was small and precise, in an old-fashioned hand. Reiko leafed through the manuscript.

"Looks like a little poem on each page. Hard to read, though. Can you make this out?"

She handed the papers to me.

"Let me see." I fished my half-glasses out of my shirt pocket and read: " 'In winter, I get up at night and dress by yellow candle-light . . . '"

Reiko's eyes widened. "I've heard that before."

"Everybody's heard that before. It's from A *Child's Garden of Verses.*

I knew 'em all by heart when I was a kid. Joanna's great-grandaddy just copied the stuff out of a book. And little Joanna, who grew up more interested in clothes and sex, had never been exposed to the original. So she bought the whole tale. I'm tempted to ask how dumb anybody can get. But, as Caesar was inclined to say, *de gustibus non est disputandum.*"

"What?"

"Roughly translated, it means that some folks like avocados, some don't."

"Oh."

The look on her face was one of puzzlement and disbelief. But she is used to me, and she merely pursed her lips and nodded her head.

"What is this, a seance?" Greg Farrell had entered the room.

"More like a wake," I said. "What are you doing here?"

I wasn't sure immediately why Greg looked so different. Then it dawned on me: He was wearing an expensive sweater—the kind Bill Cosby wears—his hair was slicked back, and his jeans had no holes in the knees. On his feet were a brand new pair of white Reeboks. In a wild surmise, I knew that he was Reiko's lunch date.

"I don't think I like this. Does this mean that there is something going on between you two?"

Reiko frowned. She looked like she was going to stamp her foot. "We're friends. We enjoy each other's company. What the hell is so wrong about that?"

"Hold it, partner. I meant no harm. If this paint-stained cave dweller will promise to take good care of you, I have no objections to your sharing an occasional meal. But, I warn you, he has a pretty shady reputation."

"Bullshit!" she said. "We are going to have a nice lunch down at the Doubletree. And I may not be back this afternoon. How do you like that?"

There was nothing left for me to say. I got up and linked arms with both of them and led them to the door. With a sad little smile, I kissed Reiko on the forehead and gravely shook hands with Greg.

"Have a good day," I said, with a blinding smile.

When they had gone, I went back to my office and sprawled in my chair. I felt blue. An old longing came back to me. I'm just not a guy who can stand to be alone—to live alone—very long. I closed my eyes.

I must have dozed. Suddenly I was aware of the scent of a very special perfume in the room, and two cool hands over my eyes. Sally Morse.

"Are you going to be around for a while now? Will I be able to get you on the phone? Are you planning on visiting me in the Valley any time soon? More to the point, do you want to buy me lunch?"

I would like to say that I rose and took her in a passionate embrace. I would like to say that we made mad love right on my desk. I would like to say that it is easy for me even to *think* of making love at 11:30 in the morning. But I won't.

But later that evening....

ABOUT THE AUTHOR

Roy Gilligan was born during the first half of the twentieth century on the south bank of the Ohio River near where the great stream admits the Licking. He was nearly famous for a very short while in Cincinnati as a TV-radio personality. In the late fifties and early sixties he wrote a weekly column on advertising for the *San Francisco Chronicle*. Later on he contributed book reviews to that same newspaper and articles to the *San Jose Mercury-News*, the *Monterey Herald*, and *San Francisco Focus* magazine, among many others. For two decades he taught English in a California high school. He lives with his first and only wife in San Jose, California. He has a daughter, Robin, who supervised the cover design of this book, two remarkable grandchildren, and sweet memories of four wonderful dogs: Wendy, Tina, Maggie, and Mandy Lou.

If you enjoyed *Poets Never Kill,* you might want to read the first two books in this series, *Chinese Restaurants Never Serve Breakfast* and *Live Oaks Also Die.*

You may order any of these books direct from the publisher. Send $8.95 plus $1.50 postage and handling to:

Brendan Books
P.O. Box 710083
San Jose, CA 95171-0083

(California residents add appropriate sales tax.)

These books are available through bookstores that use R.R. Bowker Company *Books In Print* catalog system, and distributed to the trade by Capra Press.

Critical comment on *Chinese Restaurants Never Serve Breakfast:*

"The pace of the story and the twists of the plot will hold the interest of the most jaded mystery buff."
—*Southwest Book Review*

"Gilligan's sleuth is likable, his characters (from trendy Carmelites to moneyed Pebble Beachers) ring true, and the author writes with an assured sense of irony between Carmel's charming ambience and troubled residents."

—Howard Lachtman, *The Stockton Record*

More critical comment on *Live Oaks Also Die:*

"This is a book any mystery buff will love, and it will make you want to get a copy of its predecessor, *Chinese Restaurants Never Serve Breakfast. . . .*"
—Jayne Murdock, *Small Press Exchange*

"If you liked that quirky title *Chinese Restaurants Never Serve Breakfast,* you'll love the second outing for Pat Riordan, his assistant Reiko Masuda, and the Monterey Peninsula descriptions."
—*Mystery News*

171

A MESSAGE FROM THE PUBLISHER:

When I told the author of this book that there was no way the printer could plan it out without leaving some empty pages, he said, "So leave some blank pages. Who cares?"

I said, "Maybe you could make the story a little longer." The author is a curmudgeonly fellow, and his only response was, "So I'll give you a couple of bushels of adjectives and some more commas and you can sprinkle 'em around where you please. A story is a story. It has a beginning, a middle, and an end. When it's over, it's over."

In the end, however, I was able to extract from him some words about his future projects:

The next book will feature the return of the white-haired man. He's the guy who was the henchman of the witchy old lady in *Chinese Restaurants Never Serve Breakfast*. Well, he comes back looking for something or other, and gets Riordan and Reiko involved. I think one or the other of 'em will get shot. A couple of my friends have said there's not enough gunfire in my books. Well, dammit, I'll give 'em some gunfire. Also, I've heard from a few readers who object to my people hanging around the Monterey Peninsula all the time. I should move 'em around, like Jessica Fletcher in *Murder, She Wrote*. Hey, there's enough material on the Peninsula to keep me going for years.

After that, I'm thinking of having a murder victim, maybe a famous playwright, found dead on the stage of the Forest Theatre in Carmel. The story will have to be full of off-beat characters and nasty situations. But Riordan will prevail, as always. Or he'll be pushed into prevailing by Reiko.

How's that? Think it will sell any books?

That's all I could get out of him. I suspect he has the next two books all mapped out, but he's not telling me anything.

My grandfather has told me about a series of books of which he was especially fond when he was a boy. A new one came out about every six months, and cost fifty cents in hardcover. Granddad would go into his favorite bookstore whenever he could get hold of a half dollar, take the steps to the basement where the young people's books were kept, and search the shelves. His joy on finding a new title was almost overwhelming. He would take the book to the clerk and hand over the fifty cents (there was apparently no sales tax in those days), and rush home to enjoy his treasure in one day's ecstatic read.

But there was something else that characterized that old series of stories. In the back pages of each volume were cartoons from readers as fiercely loyal as Granddad, letters from fans, even invitations to join a fan club that offered an emblem *and* a certificate. It was a way to *belong,* and it must have been a lot of fun. Books were important in those days. There was no television.

We're not suggesting a "fan club." But we would like to thank all those good folks who've read the books in our "Pat Riordan" series, and let them know that it will continue as long as our ill-tempered author can put the words on paper.

B.G. Nystedt
Publisher

There's an epidemic with 27 million victims. And no visible symptoms.

It's an epidemic of people who can't read.

Believe it or not, 27 million Americans are functionally illiterate, about one adult in five.

The solution to this problem is you... when you join the fight against illiteracy. So call the Coalition for Literacy at toll-free **1-800-228-8813** and volunteer.

Volunteer
Against Illiteracy.
The only degree you need
is a degree of caring.

Ad Council   Coalition for Literacy